❧ THE PROMISE

Peter did something really wonderful. We were talking about how we were going to break the news to our parents. I was really worried about what they were going to say. But he looked up at me with his wonderful smile and said, "Val, I don't need anyone's permission to marry you."

He pulled an envelope from his pocket and shook out a ring. He took my hand and slipped the gold band on my finger, saying, "With this ring, I, Peter Matthew Winder, marry you, Valerie Susanne Larch."

What Kind of Love?

THE DIARY OF
A PREGNANT
TEENAGER

SHEILA COLE

AN AVON  FLARE BOOK

Excerpt from "In Me, Past, Present, Future Meet" from *Collected Poems of Siegfried Sassoon.* Copyright 1918, 1920 by E. P. Dutton. Copyright 1936, 1946, 1947, 1948 by Siegfried Sassoon. Used by permission of Viking Penguin, a division of Penguin Books USA, Inc., and George Sassoon.

AVON BOOKS
A division of
The Hearst Corporation
1350 Avenue of the Americas
New York, New York 10019

Copyright © 1995 by Sheila Cole
Published by arrangement with William Morrow and Company, Inc.
Library of Congress Catalog Card Number: 94-78938
ISBN: 0-380-72575-4
RL: 6.7

First Avon Flare Printing: May 1996

AVON FLARE TRADEMARK REG. U.S. PAT. OFF. AND IN OTHER COUNTRIES, MARCA REGISTRADA, HECHO EN U.S.A.

Printed in the U.S.A.

RA   10   9   8   7   6   5   4   3   2   1

For my daughter Jennifer—
who has led me to places I have never been before.

Acknowledgments

In challenging me to understand how a young woman could decide to give her baby up for adoption, Jennifer Cole and Peg Griffin inspired me to write this book.

Although *What Kind of Love?* is a work of fiction, many of the situations described in the story are based on conversations with teenagers who have been pregnant as well as with teachers, social workers, and counselors who work with them. For their help in understanding what it is like to be young and pregnant, I am grateful to Betty Cannon, Ava Torre Bueno, and the staff of Planned Parenthood of San Diego and Riverside Counties, Fawn Martinez, Sue Schudson, Dr. Sarah Beth Hufbauer, the young women at the Victoria Summit School in San Ysidro, California and at Peninsula High School in San Bruno, California, and their teachers Linda Austin and Roberta McHue. Rosa Montes of the San Mateo County Department of Health Services, and Roy Risner, principal of Sunset High School in Encinitas, California, generously gave of their time. Sally Hufbauer was my gracious guide to the world of the young violinist.

Alice Schertle, Jonathan Cobb, Jean Ferris, Edie Gelles, Jill Norgren, Alyssa Cobb, Katie Schertle, and Susan Pearson read this book as it was taking form. Their comments, encouragement, and belief that it would make a good story kept me going through the writing and rewriting and contributed to its final form. Melanie Donovan, my editor, wrestled with my manuscript with insight, patience, and good nature. My husband, Michael Cole gave me the title and much, much more. The words *thank you* hardly seem adequate for all they have done.

Carrie was over last night, and we were making lemon bars for Mom to take to the Logicon company picnic. Nick wouldn't leave us alone. I finally chased him out of the room after he put his fingers into the bowl while I was still scraping it, but he came right back. I think Nick likes Carrie even though he's two years younger than she is. When we were playing Trivial Pursuit, he kept hanging over her shoulder and brushing her hand with his. Then, when the lemon bars were cooling, he stole one out of the pan. Carrie grabbed his wrist and they ended up wrestling for it. Carrie thought it was funny. I was mad at them both because they got gunk all over the floor. I made Nick clean it up, but he did a lousy job. The floor was sticky and Mom blamed me for it.

I want to try to get out of the picnic this afternoon so I can go to the early movie with Peter after I practice.

I drove the truck all the way down Coast Highway to Laguna Beach and back without making a single mistake! Daddy says he'll take me out on the freeway next time. He says I'm a lot easier to teach than Sandy was. She had a hard time with the gears and stalled every time she had to shift. I didn't stall once and it was only my third time driving. I'm still a little scared when other cars pass me.

On the way back, we stopped at the bakery because Daddy wanted to get some coffee. He kept pushing his Danish at me, saying, "It's delicious. Take a bite." And I kept pushing it away, saying, "Daddy, you know I'm trying to lose weight."

I wish he wouldn't keep pushing food at me. He knows I'm trying not to eat so much. But he won't take me seriously—he just laughs and hugs me and says he doesn't think skinny women are attractive. Sandy says it's because he still sees me as his little princess, running to him in my pink tutu and ballet slippers. I wish he'd realize that I'm not a little girl anymore.

It's really bugging me. I can't remember the last time I had it. I know I had it that Saturday when Peter and I rode our bikes to Dana Point. I think it was March because the acacias were in bloom, but it might have been April. I don't know. Anyway, that was months ago. I *must* have had it after that!

I almost said something about it today at school. Carrie and I were in the bathroom at lunchtime and she needed a tampon. "I wish I'd get mine," I said.

"You *still* haven't gotten it?" she said.

"You know, I'm always skipping them," I said. Although I tried to shrug it off, my face was on fire. I'm just sick about it.

Nick just stuck his head in the door to see if I want to go running with him. I'll probably feel better if I do, but it has to be a short one because I have to practice for the orchestra concert on Saturday.

Tomorrow is the French final. I've been sitting on my bed with the book open since seven o'clock. But it's no good. I can't concentrate. I keep thinking, what if. . . . No. I can't be. Not from the first time.

I knew I shouldn't have gone over to Peter's that afternoon, but I wanted to be with him so bad, I couldn't stay away. It was like there was a magnet pulling me there.

We were lying on his bed listening to a new

tape he got from Tom. At first we were just listening to the music, and then we were kind of making out, and things started to get heavy. It felt so good—we just kept going. We took off our shirts. I let him undo my bra. He was stroking my breasts and I was stroking his back. Then his hand moved down to my belly and he was easing down my pants, and then my underpants.

I could feel he was hard, and I was pulling at the buttons on his jeans, trying to undo them. I couldn't, so he undid them for me and slid them off. I know we shouldn't have, only it was too late to stop. I couldn't get enough of him. I wanted him inside me but it hurt, and when he pulled away, there was blood on my thighs. It freaked me out.

Peter kept saying he was sorry, but I was so scared. I gathered up my stuff and I got out of there as fast as I could.

I can't believe I was such a bitch to Peter. I wouldn't even talk to him for two weeks. I even glommed on to poor Mark so he would think I liked someone else. But he kept calling.

Finally I told him I didn't want to see him anymore. I loved him, but I just couldn't be with him. We were both crying, and he promised if I went back with him, we wouldn't do it again until I wanted to. He said he was miserable without me. He was saying, "I love you, I love you. You're beautiful," over and over. And we were both crying and we were kissing and everything was okay. How could I ever have thought I could stay away from him?

Dear God, I love him. Please don't let me be . . . Not now, not when everything is so good. I'm so afraid. Please let me get my period.

4

Dianne says I'm overreacting, but I know it. I failed my French final. This time I really did fail. It's because I can't keep my mind on *anything*, I'm so worried about my period. Tomorrow I have finals in both biology and geometry. I'd better pull myself together and study. I have an A going into the biology final and I can ace that, easy. But I really have to study for geometry.

I'm probably worrying for nothing. I *always* miss my period when I get upset. People do it all the time and nothing happens.

Peter came over after school, but I wanted to study and I ignored him. I know I was being awful. He didn't stay for dinner even though Mom asked him to. I felt bad after he left. I was going to call him and say I was sorry, but he called me first. I told him it was because I'm afraid I'm going to flunk geometry.

He knows me too well, though. He said, "You're mad at me, Val."

"No, I'm not," I lied. "I love you, Peter. I just can't talk about it now." I hung up on him because I was afraid that if he kept pushing me, I'd say something I'd be sorry for. I can't tell him, though. I know it's crazy, but I can't.

I can't believe what Peter did. It was wonderful. It was so romantic. He slipped a yellow rose through the door of my locker. It was there waiting for me when I came to school this morning, along with these lines from a poem by e. e. cummings.

(. . . the voice of your eyes is deeper than all roses)
nobody, not even the rain, has such small hands

I didn't know what to say to him. He made me feel really special, like he really loves me. He said I'm beautiful. He can't stand seeing me so unhappy. It makes him miserable. He wanted to know if it was something he did.

I can't tell him. It would spoil everything. And, anyhow, I don't know for sure. So I told him I love him. I was sorry about yesterday. I'm just an emotional wreck with my solo for the year-end concert coming at the same time as finals. I think he believed me. I hate myself for lying to him that way, but I can't tell him.

There's no final in English. What a relief! Mrs. Lazarson said that if we didn't already know what we should have learned in her class, we weren't going to learn it in the next few days. We're going to have a costume party instead. Everyone's bringing munchies, and we have to dress up as our favorite character from one of the books we've read this semester. At first I

6

thought, God, how immature. But it could be fun. I'm going as Juliet. I'm going to borrow Mom's teal blue velour robe and make a wreath out of baby roses and statice.

I'm bringing my killer brownies to the party, but I can't touch even one! I've been eating like a pig, and my jeans are getting tight on me. I better quit or I'll blimp out.

Thank heaven, I'm through with geometry. How am I ever going to survive trig next year? Well, have to go practice for my solo now.

I love you, Peter. I love you, Peter. I love you.

VL ☼ *PW   VL* ♡ *PW   VL* ♥ *PW   VL* ♡ *PW*

I stayed home today. I feel awful. All I want to do is sleep.

Carrie called to find out why I wasn't in school. When I told her I threw up this morning, she went on and on about how I wasn't taking care of myself and I should go to the doctor. I think she suspects something. I lied and told her I already have an appointment just to get her off my case.

I'm sorry we're not as good friends as we used to be. The two of us were like Siamese twins. We did *everything* together. She was always over here, even when I was practicing the violin, or I was over there. But things are different now that I have Peter. I know it sounds ratty, but it's true. It's not that I don't care about her. It's just not the same. I *love* Peter. And besides, I can't tell Carrie we did it. I can't tell anybody.

Would Peter tell? I'll kill him if he told Tom. If Carrie and Tom were doing it, too, maybe then I could tell her. Sometimes I think the only reason that they're together is because we are. She felt left out when I started going with Peter. She wanted a boyfriend real bad, and there was Tom in the same boat as she was.

I wonder if Carrie is wearing her new white skirt and top to Tom's party tonight. I think I'll wear my black skirt and my black tank top. I wish I had Sandy's blue and black shirt to wear

8

over it, but she took it with her to college. I've got to do something with my hair! I want to look fabulous for Peter. I think Sarah Hendrikson is after him. I saw her talking to him in the hall. Can't blame her. He *is* built. And there's his smile. All he has to do is smile and you have to smile back, no matter what.

That's what got me the first time I saw him! I can still see it. It was September 20, at orchestra practice. He stood up to play a solo on the clarinet. I thought he was cute—then he smiled, and it was like a flashbulb going off. After that, I was dying to talk to him, but I didn't have the nerve. I kept walking by where the eleventh graders sat at lunchtime, hoping he would notice me. I even made Carrie come with me a couple of times. Then, the next week, after orchestra practice, he came over to talk to me. All I could think of was what a mess I was because I had a grease stain on my shirt from lunch and I hadn't washed my hair. I was like—duh. I was sure he'd never talk to me again. But he fell into step beside me as we were leaving school and ended up walking me home. We sat on the curb in front of the house talking about music we liked. He said he liked reggae. I wasn't into it, but I pretended I liked it because I liked him. We were still talking when Mom came home from work. She made me go in and help her with dinner.

I was so embarrassed! He called me that same night and said he was going down to the San Diego Zoo on Saturday with a bunch of his friends. I was so nervous, I went on and on about how great the zoo was. Dumb-dumb that I am, it wasn't until he said, "Tell your mom she shouldn't worry. We'll be home by ten," that I finally realized he was asking me out. I walked into the sliding glass door with the telephone in my hand and almost knocked myself out. He told me afterward he'd been so afraid to call that when he heard the thump, he thought I might be hanging up on him. We haven't been apart since—except for the time after we did it. I can't believe it's been ten whole months.

Peter and I had a terrible fight last night. We went to the beach after the party. It was my fault—I know I was asking for it, but I couldn't help myself. I can't keep my hands off him. We were just kissing—then before I knew it, my panties were off and he was rolling on top of me, and all of a sudden I panicked. He was going ahead, after he promised he wouldn't. I kept punching him until he stopped.

Peter was furious. He said he didn't know why I was making such a big deal about it. It's not like I'm a virgin or we never did it before. He didn't talk to me the whole way home. He didn't even say good-night.

I know I wasn't very cool, but I'm the one who should be mad. He said we wouldn't do it if I didn't want to.

And I was right about the Sarah person. She was coming on to Peter all night. When I said something about it to him, he laughed and tried to brush it off, but I wouldn't let it go. He pulled me to him in front of everyone and kissed me really hard. "Do you think she saw that?" he whispered.

I don't care whether she did or not. She better keep her hands off him!

What if he doesn't call me? What if he calls her? I don't know what I'll do. He has to call me. Please let him call me. Please.

I didn't think things could get worse after what happened at the beach Friday, but yesterday was awful. I got up, and first I had this fight with Mom about staying out late with Peter, and then she starts on why I didn't clean the bathrooms this week or finish dusting the house. "Just because you have a boyfriend doesn't mean that you're not a member of this family anymore." According to her, I am not practicing the violin enough or doing my share around the house.

Daddy chimed in, saying, "I don't know why we're paying that character Mrs. Rykoff for your violin lessons when you don't practice. Do you realize how much those lessons cost, Val? Even electricians don't make that much an hour." I know my lessons cost a lot. He doesn't have to keep reminding me. I wish I could get a scholarship so they didn't have to pay for them.

What really bugs me is that when one of them gets on my case, the other one feels like they have to, too. There's no use explaining that I didn't have time to practice or do the cleaning last week because I had finals. It's not fair! I'm not the only one in the house who uses the bathrooms, and I don't know why I always have to be the one to clean them. I'm so tired of her getting on me about Peter. Well, maybe she won't have to worry about him anymore.

But the worst thing was, I blew my solo. I didn't come in on time and I fouled up the whole orchestra. And what made it really awful was that everyone was at the concert, including Grannie Larch and Aunt Maria and Uncle Brian. I wanted to run off the stage and hide, but I had to stay there and keep on playing. I couldn't escape. I thought I was going to burst into tears right in front of everybody.

After the concert, Aunt Maria and Uncle Brian told me they didn't even notice. They were just saying that because they're my family. Mr. Vanderhoeven wouldn't even look at me. He'll probably put me back in the third chair next year! I'll never get to play another solo. Never. All I wanted to do was go home, crawl into bed, and die. Mom and Daddy wouldn't let me, though. Mom said she wasn't going to let me make too much of it. Everyone messes up sometimes. They made me go out with them to the Old Vienna for coffee and dessert. Half the kids in the orchestra were there with their parents, including Peter and his mother. I don't know how Mom could do that to me—it was so humiliating. I hate her!

I knew he'd come back. I knew it! Peter was waiting outside to walk me to school this morning. We didn't have a chance to talk because Nick was with us. But he gave me this incredible tape and a card.

> *My lusts usurp the present tense.*
> *And strangle Reason in his seat.*
> *My loves leap through the future's fence*
> *To dance with dream-enfranchised feet.*

> *Val, that is how you make me feel. I'm sorry I got carried away and scared you. I scared myself, too. The smell of you drives me crazy. I love you, dear beautiful, fragile Valerie.*

I can't stand fighting with you, Peter. I love you. I lie in bed at night and dream of being with you, of feeling you against me. I can hardly keep from touching you when we see each other. It's scary. It's like I can't control myself.

Peter came over this evening and we decided that since we're going to keep doing it, we're going to have to start using protection. Peter didn't want to talk about it at first, but I said we had to. "We have to do something if we're not going to stop," I said.

And he went, "You said you didn't want to do it."

And I said, "I love you, Peter, and I want you

14

to love me—but I'm afraid we'll get AIDS or something."

He thought that was funny. "You're not going to get AIDS from me," he says. "There's no way I could have it."

"But I could get pregnant," I said. That stopped him. He looked like he'd just been struck by lightning. I wanted to tell him I missed my period. Since we just got back together, though, I thought it would be better not to say anything until I know for sure.

He said he'd get some condoms, but he wants me to go on the Pill.

I got a job at the nursery! I saw the Help Wanted sign on the way home from my lesson, and I went in and applied. I think Mrs. Ikura gave it to me because Daddy's such a good customer. I can't wait to tell him.

Mrs. Ikura was really nice. I told her I was going to a wedding in Chicago and I wouldn't be able to come in to work next week. She said it was okay. I could start when I got home. Mrs. Ikura wants me to learn the names of all the plants and the best conditions for growing them so I can answer customers' questions. I think I can get Daddy things there at a discount, too. He's not going to believe it. He'd given up on getting any of us interested in gardening.

I can work thirty-five hours a week or even more, if I want to. I'm going to save at least eighty dollars a week. If I can get eight hundred dollars in the bank by the end of summer, maybe Daddy will go halves on a new bow.

It's funny—after the concert Saturday, I thought I'd never feel the same about the violin again. But I had the best lesson this afternoon. We worked on the Bach I'm going to play with Grandpa Horvath at the wedding rehearsal dinner. My rhythm was better this time. In fact, the whole thing sounded good, and I feel more confident about playing it with him. He's such a perfectionist!

Mom says that I shouldn't mind Grandpa stopping me when I'm playing and telling me to do it over. He's very critical, but he means well. She's sorry she didn't understand that when she was my age. She gave up the cello because she couldn't take his criticism. She thought it was because she had no talent. She didn't realize you need honest feedback in order to improve.

Once I asked her if she was sorry she quit. She laughed and said she didn't think she was ever as good as me, but she enjoyed playing and sometimes wished she had kept up with it.

"Well, you married Daddy and had us and became a secretary," I reminded her.

She nodded. "That didn't mean I had to stop playing the cello," she said.

I know you really have to be good to become a professional like Grandpa. But I think that's what I want to do.

🌹 Wednesday, June 19

Today we found the perfect dress for me to wear to Cousin Susie's wedding. I wasn't going to try it on because it was a size too big and *way* more than we can afford. But Mom insisted and it fit like a glove. It's gorgeous. Sleeveless, with a boat neck that comes down low in back, in a dusty rose that always looks good on me. I can't wait for Peter to see me in it.

Mom said that since we're already spending a lot of money to go to the wedding, she wants us to look nice. It's going to be a *major* event. Susie's going to have four bridesmaids and Mark will have four groomsmen. And there'll be a flower girl and a ring bearer, too. Grandpa has arranged for a brass choir to play as people are seated. There will be two hundred people at the reception. Daddy says it's costing Aunt Vera and Uncle Bela a fortune.

I'd love to have a big wedding like that. I want to walk down the aisle wearing a gown with a long, long train and lots of lace and tulle that make you look like you are floating in a cloud. But I know Daddy won't go for that. He says Uncle Bela can afford to give Susie a big wedding because he's not in construction and he hasn't been hit by the recession and he didn't have to pay for her to go to college. I suppose I would rather go to college than have a big wedding.

Will Peter and I ever get married, I wonder? I can't imagine loving anyone else as much as I love him. It would be heaven to live with him. Sometimes I daydream about it. I hear his footsteps as he comes home from work in the evening and run to open the door for him, and then he catches me up in his arms and kisses me, really kisses me, so I go all soft, melting into him.

I got a *B* in French, which is better than I expected, and a *D* in geometry, which is *really* bad. I could have had an *A* in French, though, if I hadn't been so distracted that I bombed the final.

I still haven't had my period. It's never been this long before. If I don't get my period by next week, I'm going to take one of those home pregnancy tests when we're in the hotel in Chicago. I can't believe this is happening to me. Mom will kill me.

Showed Mom my report card. "This isn't very good, Valerie," she said, as if I didn't know already. Then she asked me what I planned to do about the *D*. "It isn't for me—it's for you," she said.

I feel awful when she talks to me that way. I wish she would just yell and scream. When she asks me what I'm going to do about it, she makes me feel even worse. At least she can't blame Peter for this. She knows I'm more serious about school since I started going with him. He gets mostly *A*'s. He's going to Harvard or Stanford. His parents have been planning for him to go someplace like that for college ever since he was little, and even before that. Peter says it's the only thing the two of them agree on.

Hurray! School's out! And the wedding in Chicago is next week. It will be fun, but I wish I wasn't going to be away that long from Peter. Lately he is all I think about. It is like an obsession. He's in my mind all day. At night he's in my dreams. I really have to try to balance it out. What will I do when he goes away to college?

I'm so wrapped up in Peter, I've been neglecting everybody else. Nick is mad at me. I can tell because he doesn't come and sit on my bed and talk to me like he used to. I know we hardly do anything together since I started going out with Peter, and he probably thinks I don't care about him. I do, though. I know it's weird, because most people hate their little brothers, but I really love Nick. And then there's Carrie. The other day she said straight out she thinks I only have time for her when Peter is busy. I don't know, maybe it's true. But we still have great times together, like today.

Dianne and Carrie and I got a ride over to South Coast Plaza with Dianne's sister. None of us had any money, so we were just looking.

Carrie walked into the hat store and in her terrible French asked the saleslady, *"Avez-vous le nouveau chapeau de Zozo?"* which is a line from a silly song we learned in French class. The lady didn't understand, and Carrie asked her if she had any pillboxes. When the saleslady brought her the hat, she put it on and with a perfectly straight face turned to us to ask, "Vhat do you tink, *mes chéries?* Is dis de one for Pierre?"

I cracked up. Dianne kept whispering to us, "Let's get out of here." But Carrie wouldn't leave until we tried on every hat in the store.

I saw this really cute shirt at the Limited. I can't ask Mom to buy anything right now because Daddy's business is bad. They are trying to hide it and not scare us kids, but I can tell Daddy's depressed because he's been drinking. Although he's not a drunk or anything, he has been drinking *a lot*. Sandy and I talked about it when she called last week. She said he's always like this when he doesn't have enough work. Still, it worries me.

She's going straight to Chicago from San Francisco and then we'll all fly home together—one big, happy family.

We leave tomorrow. Still haven't gotten it. I'm going to have to get the test. Damn, I'm sharing a room with Sandy. How will I hide it from her?

Oh, please, God, please let me get it before we go.

☙ Tuesday, June 25

The plane made me feel barfy. I hope it's just my stomach and nothing else.

It was a real shock to see Grandma. She's changed so much since the operation. Mom says she's a lot better than she was, but I could see that it was a real effort for Mom not to cry the whole time we were there. I'm going to try and go over Grandma's every day so I can be with her.

The wedding is Saturday. It's the first time in years that Mom's whole family and all of their kids have been together. We've been to a different house every night for dinner. They all serve this fattening Hungarian food that you have to eat to be polite. I don't think they have ever heard of low fat or low cholesterol in Chicago.

People keep calling me Sandy, even though she's three and a half years older than me and in college and she's beautiful. Now that she's back from school, she's Miss Perfect. She never does anything to make Mom and Daddy mad. I used to hate her because she has Mom's tiny nose and I wish I had it. Mine is like Daddy's and comes straight down from my forehead like the Statue of Liberty's. But Peter thinks it has character. He loves it. Anyhow, I can't understand how people could get us mixed up. We're so different.

I was going to talk to Sandy, but I decided not to. She thinks she knows everything. And she's so bossy to Nick and me—like on Sunday,

23

Aunt Vera was serving dessert and she wouldn't let her give me any. She said I was getting fat. And then on Monday, when I said I didn't want to go window-shopping with her because I wanted to take a nap before dinner, she asked me if I was practicing for the role of Sleeping Beauty. I can't believe I ever missed her. What a bitch!

On the other hand, Daddy is being great. I think he's trying to keep us out of Mom's way so she can spend all her time with Grandma. Yesterday when Mom went with Grandma to the doctor, he took me and Nick to this Chinese restaurant for lunch. It looked like a dump, but the food was wonderful. Then we went to this music store that had *everything*, and he said we each could choose one thing. I picked Rachmaninoff's Second, even though I don't think I'll be able to play it. It's so romantic, though.

Today we went sailing on Uncle Bela's boat. Daddy let us all take turns steering the boat. We were going fast, and the boat was keeling until I was almost in the water. Sandy was screaming, "It's going to turn over. Stop, Daddy! Stop!" But Daddy just laughed.

When it was Nick's turn, he almost sailed us right into a big tour boat. Daddy kept yelling at him, "Turn your tiller. More to starboard, away from you, more, more." We would have rammed into the other boat if Daddy hadn't grabbed the tiller away from him at the last minute. The captain of the boat waved his fist at us. Nick and I thought it was hilarious. Sandy was furious and said she'd never get in a boat with us again.

Nick said he wouldn't have hit it. He only

wanted to see how close he could come. He would have turned away at the last minute. I thought Daddy was going to bawl Nick out, but he just took over and didn't let Nick take the tiller again.

It was fun. Daddy says if we really want to learn how to sail, he'll take us out in the harbor at Newport Beach. They rent boats there. I would love to go sailing with Peter. Only five more days until I see him again. I wish I were in his arms right now.

I bought the home pregnancy test kit this morning on my way over to see Grandma. I was terrified. They were on the shelf right under the partition for the area where they fill prescriptions, and I know the druggist was watching me. I grabbed a test and walked to the register. I thought someone might say something or give me a look, but no one did. I just paid for the test, put it in my backpack, and walked out.

I know the man behind the desk was watching me. I could feel his eyes on me the whole time I was waiting for the elevator. It made me feel real self-conscious. As soon as I was in the room, I put the kit in with all of my dirty clothes where no one will look. I don't want to take it now because Sandy will be back any minute and I might still get my period.

I practiced with Grandpa today, and now I understand why Mom quit. He was working with me on my bowing and kept yelling, "More tone, more tone, louder." It was exhausting. He really is hypercritical. He kept stopping me and making me play every passage over again. Whenever I messed up, he shouted, "No! No! Not that way!" Then he would do it so I could hear how it was supposed to sound.

Afterward, when we were having tea with Grandma, Grandpa told me that if I want to be a violinist, nothing should matter to me right now except my music. It has to come before everything. "None of this sex business," he said. "All of your energy and passion should go into your music if you want to be good. Save the sex for later."

I had a hard time keeping a straight face when he said that. But I have to admit he's probably right that I'm going to have to concentrate and work on my playing if I want to make it.

The duet with Grandpa this evening was a giant success. I was good. Even Grandpa, who hardly ever says anything good about anyone's playing, said so. Daddy was crying, though he'd never admit it. He said he just had something in his eye.

Oh, please, dear God, let me not be pregnant. It would hurt Mom and Daddy so much.

I'm pregnant! The test was positive. I did it in the bathroom this morning when Sandy went to help Susie get ready. My hand was shaking so badly I could hardly read it, but it was pink, pink for positive. What am I going to do? I can't be pregnant. I'm only fifteen!

I took off all of my clothes, and looked at myself in the mirror. My breasts are big, bigger than they have ever been, and feel heavy and hard. My nipples are darker, too. My stomach is not as flat as it used to be, either, and it will get bigger.

I can't go to the wedding. I can't face them.

I told Mom I had a headache and came upstairs to the room after the reception started. I just wanted to die. I went out on the balcony and I climbed over the rail. I stared down twenty-three stories to the street in front of the hotel. I wanted to jump, but I couldn't do it. I climbed back onto the balcony and sat there for hours. Then everyone from the reception came pouring out of the hotel. The crowd parted, and the bride and bridegroom rushed out, holding hands. Everyone was crowding around, throwing rice at them, and they were ducking and laughing. Mark opened the car door for Susie. She stopped to throw her wedding bouquet into the crowd and then got into the car. Mark leaned down and kissed her before he closed the door.

I'll never be in a scene like that now. You don't have big weddings when you're pregnant. You just get married, if you're lucky. But Peter won't want to get married because he has all these plans for what he's going to do—like college and med school. I don't know what to do. Soon everyone will know.

❧ Monday, July 1

Why doesn't he call? I called him as soon as we got home yesterday and left a message. What if he stopped loving me while I was gone? What if he found someone else, like Sarah? Even though he says he's not interested, she's beautiful and she wants him. He can't like Sarah. I need him. He has to love me. He can't leave me to face this by myself. It's his fault. I wouldn't be pregnant if it wasn't for him.

❧ Tuesday, July 2

He called. His grandmother had a stroke. He is staying with his grandfather. I didn't say anything, but he could tell something was wrong. I said I couldn't talk about it on the phone. I'd tell him when he got back on Thursday.

I don't know how I'll make it till then.

Today was my first day at the nursery. It was okay, considering. . . . We were so busy, I didn't have time to think about anything.

❧ Wednesday, July 3

Went to work. Dianne and I played tennis after work. She won. I'm really not very good. I wonder why she even plays with me. She wanted me to come over and go swimming afterward. I said I couldn't. My breasts have gotten so big, I'm popping out of my bikini and I'm afraid she'll notice. I wonder if people can tell yet. I can't stand this. I wish Peter were here.

Everyone went to the Jacobsens' Fourth of July party except me. I told them I didn't want to go. Daddy grumbled about it, but Mom said I'd ruin it for them if they had to force me. Peter came over right after they left. I was so scared, I started to cry when he walked in the door.

All the color left his face as soon as I told him. He didn't want to believe me and he asked me again, hoping, I guess, that I would say I was just joking. He looked like he was going to cry when I said I was serious. "You have to do something, Val," he said.

That got me, and suddenly I was yelling at him, "*You* have to do something about it. It's your fault. You wanted to do it."

I was sorry the minute the words were out of my mouth. We sat there without saying anything. Then he got up to go. He said he'd figure something out.

He started for the door. All at once he turned around and grabbed me up in his arms and held me to him so tight I could feel his heart pounding against me. We stood there holding each other for a long time. I don't know how long. I wanted to do it because then I'd know he loved me. But he didn't. He was shaking and he just wanted to be held.

I felt empty and sad when he left. I looked through the photo albums. There was a picture of Daddy and me climbing up Piute Pass in the Sierras last summer. Daddy thinks I'm his sweet little girl, his princess. What will he think of me now?

Suddenly I had to get out of there. I couldn't stand being in the house—their house—anymore. I took my bike, just riding around, going nowhere. That was me, going nowhere—I didn't realize I'd swerved into a car until I hit the pavement.

The driver of the car stopped. He was shouting at me, "Are you crazy?" The woman who was behind him got out of her car. "It's not my fault," he said, pointing at me. "She rode into me."

"Oh, shut up. Can't you see she's hurt?" another man said, rushing up behind her. He put his arm around me and made me sit down on the curb and told me his wife was calling an ambulance.

I said I was okay, but no one was listening to me, and I was afraid that the ambulance was going to come. I grabbed my bike and took off before anyone could stop me. The front fender was bent out of shape, and it scraped the tire all the way home.

Mom and Daddy made a fuss when they got home and saw me. I told them I hit something on the road and fell. And they believed me, their dear, good little girl. I hate myself. I wish I were dead.

Peter and I drove to the park this evening to talk about it. It was another bad scene. When we got there, we saw all of these homeless people. There must have been sixty of them in the parking lot—all ages, even kids. They stood around in small groups of twos and threes. Usually, with that many people in one place, there's a hum, but it was quiet, so quiet.

A truck pulled into the parking lot, and they all crowded around it. The people in the truck had a bullhorn that echoed so I couldn't catch what was said, but it must have been an order to line up, because that is what they did. Then someone opened the gate of the truck and began handing out food.

There was this girl who was fifteen or sixteen, my age. She was carrying a baby in one arm and had a dirty bedroll slung on her back. She didn't seem to be with anyone. Did she run away? Was she kicked out of her house because of the baby? Will they kick me out?

After the people left, Peter and I got out of the car and walked down the hill to the swings. I asked him if he'd told anyone about it. He said no. I didn't believe him. He got all upset and said I was being crazy. "If we don't do something about it soon, everyone will know. So what does it matter who I told? It was only my cousin Beth. She won't tell anyone."

Of all the people! His cousin Beth! She has the biggest mouth in the whole world. I couldn't

35

believe he'd done that. I was so upset, I got off the swing and ran out of the playground. Peter ran after me and grabbed me by the arm. "You want me to take care of it. Well, I am," he shouted. He was hurting my arm and I was crying.

He led me to a picnic bench. We sat there until I calmed down. He said his cousin Beth was disgusted with him for not using condoms. She told him I should go to Planned Parenthood. I don't need an appointment there, and they'll arrange for me to get an abortion. She's loaning him the money to pay for it.

He thinks it's so simple. You just walk in, put down your money, and it's all over in a few minutes. He doesn't know what he's talking about. He can tell me that it's safe, but it's me who has to do it, not him.

❧ Sunday, July 7

I never said I'd get an abortion! All I said was I would find out about it. Peter thinks that because I said I'd go to Planned Parenthood with him on Friday, I'm going to have one. I don't want to. I don't know what else to do, though.

❧ Monday, July 8

Last night I had a nightmare. I dreamed I had the abortion and I died, and Planned Parenthood had to call Mom and Daddy and tell them.

Peter says people don't die during a legal abortion in a clinic. But he only knows what his cousin Beth says, and she just wants to get him out of this. She doesn't care about me.

I wish Carrie weren't in Montana so I could talk to her about it. At least she cares what happens to me.

❦ Tuesday, July 9

I was going to call and cancel my lesson for today because I didn't think I'd be able to concentrate and it would be a waste. But I forgot and had to go. Mrs. Rykoff was wearing another one of her ethnic costumes. I think it was from Afghanistan or someplace like that. Once we got into the music, it wasn't bad. She said, "Vonderful . . . O-o-oh, zat iz nice, very nice, my dear," when I played the Vivaldi. And I didn't have to do the Kreutzer exercises, which was a giant relief because they are *so* boring. Then we started work on the Bach. She made me take the slow movement apart, counting very carefully. "Now leesten, my dear. Leesten carefully," she kept telling me. It *is* gorgeous.

If I don't go to Planned Parenthood on Friday, Peter won't speak to me again. I wish it would go away without my doing anything. Why can't I just have a miscarriage?

Peter's grandmother died last night. He went to Los Angeles for the funeral. I really shouldn't be so selfish, but when he told me, I kept thinking, why did she have to go and die now? I finally got myself all psyched up to go to Planned Parenthood and now I can't. I can't go by myself. I'm too scared.

Poor Peter! He loved her. He says that his grandma and grandpa were the only nice people in his father's family. His grandma always made him these chocolate pecan cookies. And every holiday—even St. Patrick's Day and Halloween—she sent him and Mike these silly cards and ten dollars each to buy themselves a treat.

Grandma will probably die soon, too, because of the cancer. I wish I could call her and tell her how much I love her. Daddy would have a fit if I called Chicago, though, because we just saw them.

I had today off, but Peter's still in Los Angeles. The one person around was Dianne. She was only going over to the recycling center where she's volunteering this summer, but I went with her, anyway.

We talked about Peter's grandmother. Dianne says she's afraid she'll die young and never get a chance to really live. I think she feels like she's missing out because she hasn't ever had a boyfriend. She told me she was jealous of me and Peter. Boy! If she only knew!

I didn't let anything slip, I know I didn't, but somehow Planned Parenthood came up. "Lily went there to get the Pill," Dianne told me, all wide-eyed and prissy.

Sometimes Dianne is so naive! *Lots* of kids get birth control. I wouldn't be in this mess if I had. But I didn't think we'd go all the way. I told Dianne I thought Lily was smart to be prepared. Then she asked if I thought Arianna and Will were doing it. "Duh!" I said.

And she goes, "No!" like I'd shot her straight through the heart. Dianne's such a baby.

She said she saw Tom at the beach with Molly Stein yesterday, and she was going to write Carrie to tell her. I told her not to, and she'd better not, because it will ruin Carrie's vacation. Dianne says we have to let her know because we're her friends. I don't think you have to tell your friends *everything*.

❧ Monday, July 15

I'm going to die. I know it. Something is going to go wrong.
Peter, please come home. I need you.

❧ Tuesday, July 16

At work today, Mrs. Ikura showed me how to shape azaleas when they get too leggy. Now I can do the ones along the side of the house. But I need to practice the violin first.
No word from Peter.

HE'S BACK! Peter was waiting when I got off work today. I was so glad to see him I just wanted to be alone somewhere with him, but he made me go back in and tell Mrs. Ikura I can't come in tomorrow. Then he said he had to leave, that his mother was meeting him at the bank in ten minutes to sign some papers.

We're going tomorrow. I wish it were over with.

I *knew* something would go wrong. I'm four months pregnant. *FOUR MONTHS!* And if I want to have an abortion, I have to do it in the hospital. And it takes two days and costs eight hundred dollars or more.

It was a nightmare. The place was mobbed when we got there. I didn't want everyone to hear, so I whispered to the woman at the desk, "I'm here for an abortion." She didn't hear me, and I had to say it louder. Everybody was looking at me. It was so humiliating.

She gave me this form to fill out with all these questions, like how many abortions (abortions!) I'd had, things like that. Because there was no place left to sit, I had to stand and Peter went outside to wait. I would have gone outside with him, but I was afraid they'd call my name and I wouldn't hear.

They sent me to the bathroom with a cup to pee in. I was so nervous, I ended up going all over my hand and the toilet seat. I knew I was pregnant, but I kept hoping that maybe I was wrong. When the counselor told me the test was positive, I felt like I'd been punched in the chest, and I started to cry. I couldn't help it. She handed me a box of Kleenex and waited for me to stop crying.

The counselor asked me about when I had my last period, if I really wanted an abortion—stuff like that—and I started crying all over again. She asked me if I wanted Peter to come in, and

43

when she brought him in a minute later, he wouldn't even look at me. He didn't say a word when she told him I was pregnant. He just slumped down in the chair.

The counselor took out this little paper wheel and showed us that I'd be about sixteen weeks pregnant if my last period was in March. I have to see their nurse practitioner on Monday to confirm how many weeks pregnant I am.

Then she told us an abortion would take two days and cost somewhere between six hundred and fifty and eight hundred and twenty-five dollars, depending on whether I was in my fifteenth or sixteenth week. Peter said he thought it would cost two hundred and fifty dollars. The counselor told us that's only during the first three months of pregnancy. She said we can apply to Medi-Cal if we don't have the money, but they may try to give us a runaround. She said a lot of other things—I can't remember it all. She gave me a lot of stuff to read, too. I left it in Peter's car.

Peter still wouldn't look at me when we left. I tried to take his hand, but he pulled away from me. He didn't say a word. Then, when we got on the freeway, he exploded. "Four months, Val!" he yelled. "Why didn't you say something before now? How long have you known?"

I wanted to answer, but I was crying so hard I couldn't say anything. After I stopped crying, I told him I was sorry. I told him he shouldn't worry because I was going to kill myself. And then he said if I was going to kill myself, he would kill himself, too. Then I was telling him about the balcony in the hotel in Chicago, and I got this crazy image of the two of us jumping out of a window holding hands like Superman and Lois Lane, and I was laughing and crying at the same time.

"It's not funny, Val," he said.

We pulled off at the beach so we could talk about it seriously. He kept telling me that *I* should go to Medi-Cal to apply for the money so *I* could get an abortion. I didn't say anything. It was boiling hot in the car and he was mad. He said if I wasn't going to be reasonable, he was going to go in the surf and cool off and I could sit there and cook if I wanted.

I was in the water a minute later. I was really dreading going home, and for a few minutes while I was swimming, it was such a relief not to think about it.

I was sure they'd know the minute they laid eyes on me. Instead, as soon as I walked in the door, Mom went ballistic because I missed dinner and didn't call. She went on and on about how inconsiderate I was and how I didn't give a damn about anyone but myself. How I didn't care that she and Daddy were killing themselves trying to put food on the table and pay the bills.

I just stood there, listening to her yell at me and thinking that if she acts like this when all I did was miss dinner, what will she do when she finds out I'm pregnant? When she was finished with me, I said I was sorry I was late and I went to my room and shut the door.

Daddy came in a few minutes later. He said he thought I was old enough to understand what's going on. He told me Mom's exhausted from work and worried that he's going to lose his business. He said we were going to have to make a lot of cuts in the budget until he gets more work. He asked me if I would mind taking a break from the violin. It's only for the summer. They're going to try to come up with the money to pay for lessons in the fall. I said it was okay, and I told Daddy I'd do the cooking a couple of times a week to help out.

It really is okay. I don't feel right about taking anything from them, especially now. And I don't want to get into any fights with them.

I had this pelvic exam. It was awful. The nurse said it was the only way to tell how far along I am. My feet were in these stirrup things to keep my legs apart during the exam. Then she put her hand in me. It was the most humiliating experience I've ever had.

After it was over, I went to talk to the counselor again. She told me I'm due at the end of December and asked me what I wanted to do. I said I didn't know, I had to talk to my boyfriend. She said she'd get him, but I said I wanted to talk to him alone.

When I came out to the car, Peter took one look at me and said, "It's too late, isn't it?" I didn't answer and he said, "We're going right over to the welfare office to apply for Medi-Cal."

I asked him if he'd let me think about it. He said that I couldn't keep waiting—and hoping that some miracle would happen. If I hadn't waited so long already, I wouldn't be in this mess.

"*You* got me into it," I said. "If you—"

He turned the key in the ignition and pulled out so fast the tires squealed. We didn't say another word to each other the whole way there. When we pulled into the parking lot at the welfare office, he reached across me and opened the door without saying anything. He stayed in the car.

In the office, I asked the woman at the desk

for an application for Medi-Cal assistance. She asked who it was for. I said it was for me, and she asked why I needed it. As soon as she heard what it was for, she started asking me these questions—like, do your parents know, who supports you, those kinds of things. Then she said that if I was living at home with my parents, I wasn't eligible for Medi-Cal assistance unless they qualified.

I told her the counselor at Planned Parenthood said that Medi-Cal wouldn't tell my parents. And she said no, that wasn't true. Unless I declared myself an emancipated minor, they needed to know what my family's income was. I got up and walked out, leaving her sitting there with her applications and forms.

Peter didn't believe me when I told him what happened. It really burned me. I said, "If you think you can do better, go apply yourself." That shut him up.

I'm such a screwup. I can't believe it. Mrs. Rykoff waited half an hour today before she decided I wasn't coming. I meant to call and tell her. I feel terrible.

To make it even worse, I had to tell her I wasn't going to take lessons this summer. She said I was making real strides in my playing, and I'd lose the momentum if I stopped now. I promised her that I'd practice. She asked if the money was a problem. I said no, that wasn't it, because I knew Mom and Daddy would be mad if I said anything. I told her I just needed to take a rest.

I *was* making real progress with her, and I feel bad about stopping. But I probably would never have made it as a professional, anyway. There's so much competition.

We made up! Peter called at seven. He never came out and said he was sorry, but I could tell he was because he said he was just calling to let me know he loves me and he would never let me go through this alone. He said there's something he wants to talk to me about, but he doesn't want to do it on the telephone.

I have a feeling that he's going to ask me to marry him. It's what I've been praying for. It would make everything all right.

There's this amazingly beautiful piece for violin and orchestra on the radio right now. It's so sad and beautiful, with wonderful soaring passages that I'd *love* to play. The announcer just said that it is *The Lark Ascending* by Ralph Vaughan Williams. Got to get the music.

I still can't believe it's really happening. Mrs. Winder! Me, Valerie Larch-Winder! Peter came by to drive me to work this morning. That's when he proposed. He parked a few blocks from here, leaned over, and said, "I think we should get married, Val." He told me he loved me and wanted to be with me for the rest of his life, and I was crying. All I ever seem to do now is cry.

We talked about the baby. It's the first time we ever talked about it, really. Before, it was *it*, but now that we're getting married, it's *Our Baby*. When I asked him if he wanted a boy or a girl, he got this marvelous look on his face. "I want a daughter. A little girl, with a funny nose and sapphire blue eyes like yours," he said. I just hope it has Peter's smile and his nose, not mine.

I didn't want to leave him, but I had to. It felt weird waiting on people at the nursery as if nothing had happened. All the time I was working, I was thinking, Peter and I are getting married, Peter and I are getting married, Peter and I are getting married. It was like a song in my head. Mrs. Ikura asked me what I was so happy about. "You must be in love," she said. I laughed.

Peter did something really wonderful. I was sitting at the counter in his kitchen watching him make a tuna sandwich. We were talking about how we were going to break the news to our parents. I was really worried about what they're going to say. But he looked up at me with his wonderful smile, put down the fork, and said, "Val, I don't need anyone's permission to marry you. We *are* married, as married as we'll ever be." He pulled an envelope from his pocket and shook out a ring. Coming around to my side of the counter, he took my hand and slipped the wedding ring on my finger, saying, "With this ring, I, Peter Matthew Winder, marry you, Valerie Susanne Larch."

I cried. Peter held my face in his hands and kissed me. He kissed my eyelids and the tears on my lashes, saying I shouldn't cry. We split the tuna sandwich, ate half of a coffee cake that was in the fridge, and finished off the milk. And then we went upstairs. He undressed me, kissing me softly, moving his lips slowly down my body. Then I undressed him and tortured him with my kisses. I never got as far as his feet— we couldn't wait. It wasn't anything like the first time because now I wanted it and it felt right. It was incredible, really incredible. I wish we could have stayed there together forever.

Although the ring is just a gold band, I think it's lovely. I keep twirling it around on my finger and holding out my hand and looking at it.

I wish I didn't have to take it off, but I don't want to tell Mom and Daddy tonight. I'll do it tomorrow when I get home from work.

It's amazing. I'm going to marry Peter and we're going to have a baby, a real live baby! The three of us will do everything together. I know it will be hard because we don't have any money and the baby will be a big responsibility. But it's going to be okay.

I started working on *The Lark*. Peter, my own dear, thoughtful Peter, bought the music for me.

We were just sitting down to dinner when the phone rang. Daddy answered. All he had to say was, "What? They're what?" And then he looked at me in this awful way, and I knew. I got up from the table and ran to my room.

Mom was right after me. Asking me what was going on. Telling me to turn around to face her. Then Daddy burst in. "She's pregnant! Four months pregnant!" He pushed Mom away and started smacking me.

Mom kept yelling, "Stop it, Dave! Stop it!" over and over. And suddenly he stopped. When I looked up, he was gone.

Mom sat down beside me and put her arm around me, and it all just came out. I told her everything: that I'm pregnant and that Peter and I want to get married.

She said that the call was from Peter's mother, and Mrs. Winder wasn't about to give Peter permission to get married. She said she wasn't sure it was a good idea, either. We sat there for a few minutes without saying anything. I kept wishing I could cry, as if that would make it better, but I couldn't. I was shaking so bad.

Mom said she didn't think we were going to solve the problem right then. She had to think about it some more. She went into the kitchen, and I went to the bathroom to wash my face. When I came out, she was clearing away the dinner no one had touched. Daddy's truck was gone, and Nick and Sandy had scattered. Run for cover.

Daddy came slamming in while I was washing the dishes. Mom said we had to talk. He said, "What is there to talk about? We should have done our talking to her a long time ago." He poured himself some scotch and went into the living room. Mom followed him, and I finished the dishes and went back to my room. I could hear their voices but not what they were saying. I wanted to call Peter, but I was afraid his mother would answer. I just sat there on my bed, frozen.

At about ten o'clock, I heard Sandy and Nick come in. A few minutes later Sandy came into my room. For a minute, we just looked at each other without saying anything, and then I started crying because I knew she was going to tell me that it was dumb for me to let myself get pregnant. Instead, she came and put her arms around me and said, "Why didn't you tell me? I would have helped." She offered to sleep with me if it would make me feel better. I said it was okay, that she could sleep in her own bed. I didn't think I would be able to sleep.

It was almost midnight when I heard Mom rush down the hall to their room and slam the door behind her. I went to the kitchen to get a drink of water. I was sitting at the table, and Daddy came in. He didn't even look at me. He went to the cupboard to get the scotch bottle. Then he walked back into the living room, turned on the TV, and started switching channels. I came back in here about an hour ago. It's almost three o'clock and I can still hear him out there.

I wish I were dead.

They were both waiting for me when I came into the kitchen. Mom said she'd called the nursery and told them I was sick, and then started in by telling me how much faith they'd had in me and how I'd disappointed them both. Then it was Daddy's turn. "I used to listen to the guys at work tell me how rotten their kids were," he said. "And I'd think, not me. Not me. I'm lucky. My kids are good. I was always telling them how wonderful you are. A violinist. A real talented kid. And now you've gone and gotten yourself pregnant and made a monkey out of me. I can't look anyone in the face. I'm too ashamed. I don't know how I'm going to tell your grandmother about this. She was so proud of you." He looked like he was going to cry.

I tried to tell him I was sorry, but he didn't want to hear. He said I was a little whore and asked me how many other guys I was doing it with. I got up to leave, but he shoved me back into the chair.

"I'm talking to you," he yelled. "You've ruined your life, and you're only fifteen."

"It's done, Dave," Mom said. "She's pregnant. Now we have to decide what to do about it."

I told them Peter and I had already decided what to do. We loved each other and we were going to get married.

"You're too young to get married," Mom interrupted.

"You were young when you got married," I reminded her.

"We were nineteen and twenty-one, not fifteen and seventeen," Daddy shouted. "And we're not talking about us—we're talking about you, Valerie. I'm not giving you permission to get married to that rotten little son of a bitch. I could kill him for what he's done to you. It's bad enough without you throwing your life away and getting married to him."

Then he went on about how they were trying to think of some way to salvage my life so I can finish high school, grow up and make something of myself. *Salvage* was the word he used. Like I was a wrecked car. He said if it wasn't too late, I had to get an abortion. Otherwise, he'd have to send me away somewhere. They don't understand. It's not up to them. It's up to me and Peter.

Peter called. I knew it was him because Mom slammed the receiver down without saying anything. I told her it was my phone call and she had no business hanging up on him. She turned her back on me.

I didn't think Mom would let me go to work today, but she did. I was so glad to get out of that house. They hate me. I can see it in the way they look at each other when I come into the room. They don't have to say anything. I should just run away. I have to talk to Peter. Maybe we'll both run away.

The only person I'd miss in this family is Nick. Yesterday, when Mom and Daddy were treating me like dirt, he came into my room and asked me if I wanted to hear his new tape.

I asked him if he hated me for getting pregnant. He shook his head no. "Even if the other kids talk about me and tease you because of me?"

He didn't answer right away. He just looked at me. Then, with a perfectly straight face, he said, "I'll belt anybody who opens his mouth," and he put up his fists and socked me on the arm, softly, kidding around, and I socked him back in the chest. "You wanna fight about it?" he said, and suddenly he had me by the arm and I was on the floor and we were wrestling. It felt so good, so like things used to be. Afterward I picked up the violin and played for two hours straight.

They've talked to Mom's gynecologist about my getting an abortion. He says he won't do it because I'm too far along. So they have decided the only thing for me to do is give my baby up for adoption.

When they told me that, I blew up. "You're telling me that I'm supposed to have this baby and then give it away? You're crazy. If you think I'm going to do that, you're crazy."

"Are you really prepared to raise a baby by yourself?" Mom asked. Before I could answer, she continued, "You'd better get this straight, Valerie. We're in no position to help you, and even if we had the money we wouldn't. It'd only help you ruin your life." She went on and on about how smart and talented I am and what a wonderful future I could have if I wasn't saddled with a baby. "You could get an education and finish school and you could play the violin."

I couldn't believe it. "You want me to give away my baby just so I can go to school and take violin lessons, which we can't afford, anyway?" I shouted. I tried to tell them that they didn't understand anything, that what Peter and I had was love. But they wouldn't listen.

Mom said that love wouldn't take me very far at the grocery store or with the landlord. "Get real," she said. "You can't raise a child by yourself, and there is no way Daddy and I are going to do it for you."

59

Dr. Price told them that he could make all the arrangements. Wow! Isn't that nice and convenient? All I have to do is be pregnant for the next five months and give birth, and then poof! We can all pretend it never happened.

I tried all day yesterday to get hold of Peter.
I even left a message at the lifeguard station
where he works. I was going crazy. I kept thinking, why didn't he call? What happened to him?
Then last night I couldn't stand not knowing
anymore. I waited until everyone was in bed,
then slipped out of the house. I rode my bike
over to Peter's. It seemed as if it took forever,
like I was pedaling my bike in slow motion. The
lights were still on at his house when I got there.
I sat on the curb a few doors away and waited.
It was so quiet I could hear the cars on the freeway. I was shivering.

Finally the lights went out. I waited awhile to
make sure everyone was asleep, and then tip-
toed around the side of the house to Peter's window. The window was partially open, but I
couldn't climb up to it. I was ready to turn
around and go back home, when I decided to
try the sliding glass doors to the patio. One of
them opened, and I crept up the stairs to Peter's
room. In the dark, I could barely make out Peter
lying facedown on the bed. I leaned over and
kissed him on his neck and back and whispered
in his ear. He shuddered and then rolled his
head to one side and was awake, asking me
what I was doing and hugging and kissing me
all at the same time. "You're crazy," he kept
saying over and over.

I was shivering so hard, I could hardly talk.
He shushed me and pulled me down onto the

bed and pulled the covers over me. He ran his hand up and down my back until I was no longer shaking.

I knew he didn't tell his mother. She found the receipt from Planned Parenthood in the pocket of his jeans when she was doing the laundry. Then she searched his room and found the receipt for the wedding ring. She confronted him when he came home from work. He tried to tell her some story about helping one of the guys he works with, but she didn't believe him. He had to tell her the truth. He said she threw a fit and said all sorts of awful things. She made him promise he wouldn't see me and threatened to throw him out if he did.

I told him what had happened at my house, but I really didn't feel like talking because his hand was inside my panties and I wanted to take them off.

We must have fallen asleep after we made love. It was just starting to get light out when I woke up. When I made a move to go, Peter pulled me back into bed. The next thing I knew, it was six-thirty! I could hear Mrs. Winder moving around downstairs.

Out of the corner of my eye, I saw Mrs. Winder standing at the stove with her back to me as I crept down the stairs. I slipped out the front door and pulled my bike out of the bushes. I was afraid someone would see me coming in. But nobody did. Everything was like it always is. Daddy's truck was already gone, and Mom, Sandy, and Nick were still asleep. They never suspected I was gone.

❧ Saturday, August 3

This morning Mrs. Ikura had me deadheading the flowers. It was hot, and bending over made me dizzy. I thought I was going to faint. As soon as I finished, I hid myself in the potting shed where it's cool and made myself look real busy.

Carrie called when I was practicing *The Lark* this afternoon. I didn't want to talk to her, but she said she knew something was the matter because she had called three times and Mom told her I couldn't come to the phone. I was so mad, I ended up telling her everything: how Mom and Daddy don't give a damn about me, how they wish I'd disappear so they won't have to tell their friends, and that they're going to send me away if they can. Daddy even said as much. When I told her my parents want me to give the baby away, she said, "It's your own flesh and blood. You can't do that," and I thought she really understood. But then she couldn't believe I got pregnant the first time we did it. When I told her that Peter and I are getting married, she started shrieking, "You're going to get married? Married? You can't be," and I realized she didn't understand at all.

"Why not?" I asked.

"Because you're only fifteen and Peter's seventeen. No one gets married at fifteen," she said. That made me mad, and I told her *we* were going to.

But even if she doesn't really understand, I'm glad she's back from vacation. She's still my best friend.

Today was my day off and Mom took me to see Dr. Price. She was so uptight the whole way there that I almost told her to stop the car and let me out. But once I got inside with Dr. Price, it wasn't so bad. He didn't act like he was shocked, and he didn't lecture me, except about my diet: He says I've got to eat more fruit, vegetables, and dairy products. He wants me to have an ultrasound so he can tell for sure how far along I am and whether the baby is developing normally. That was about it, except that I had another pelvic exam. Ugh!

I was in my room after dinner, when the doorbell rang. I heard Daddy say, "Carrie," and I came tearing out of my room. I was out the door before he had a chance to say no.

It wasn't until Carrie pulled away from the curb that I realized *she* was driving the car. I'd forgotten her birthday was last week. I'd been so wrapped up in my own problems, I hadn't even sent her a birthday card! Carrie said it was okay. She was going to tell me when she called that she'd passed her driver's test on the very first try, but when I told her what was happening to me she totally forgot.

We were so glad to see each other and talking so fast that I didn't pay attention to where we were going until we pulled up in front of Tom's house. I was so happy when I saw Peter's car. I was squealing. But I knew something was wrong as soon as I saw him.

"What is it?" I asked.

"What it is," Tom said, giving me this look, "is that Peter has to go live with his dad, and it's our senior year."

Peter said his mom was afraid we'd still see each other, so she's making him live with his dad in Santa Barbara. But he's not going. He said he loved me and he wasn't going to let our parents keep us apart. He wants us to go to Las Vegas. His cousin Beth says you don't need your parents' permission to get married there.

We were just beginning to get excited about

Las Vegas when Tom pointed out that we were going to need someplace to live because our parents would probably throw us out. Carrie offered to lend us the money so we could rent our own place. With the money Peter and I have saved from our jobs this summer, it should be enough.

I can't believe it. It's all happening so fast. Peter will look for a place for us to live this weekend. Then on Tuesday we're off to Las Vegas to get married. I wish Tom and Carrie could come with us, but of course they can't. They'd both get in trouble if they did, and besides, Tom has to work. I'm sorry they won't be there with us—they are such good friends. I love them. I love Peter.

We're really going to do it! I'm so excited. I keep thinking about what to wear, which is really dumb. I wonder if I can still get into the dress I wore to Susie's wedding. I have to try it on.

🌿 Friday, August 9

Carrie's having a party for us. Her parents are going to L.A. Monday and won't be home until late. It's sweet of her, although I'm afraid everyone will be freaked out by our getting married. I don't know why I should care so much what other people think, but I do. I wonder whether we should tell them I'm pregnant or just say we're getting married. I guess it would be dumb not to say anything about it. They'll all know soon enough.

I wonder if people can tell yet. I'm not really sticking out very much. I just don't have a waist in front anymore.

Only thirty-eight hours to go, and we'll be married. Peter stopped by the nursery today. He thinks he's found an apartment! It's over a garage and it's tiny. There's a backyard the owners might let us use, though. We'd have to take care of the yard, but that isn't anything. I have my fingers crossed that they'll let us have it.

We have it all planned. I've asked Mrs. Ikura if I can take Tuesday off. In the morning I'll act like I'm going to work. I'll ride my bike over to Carrie's, and Peter will pick me up there. It takes about five hours to drive to Las Vegas from here. Carrie says there are big signs for wedding chapels all over the place, so it will be real easy to find one. We already have the ring, and Carrie's buying the flowers. I packed the dress and shoes I'm going to wear at the wedding and hid them out in the garage.

Carrie called. She said Peter was trying to get hold of me last night, but the line was busy and then Mom answered and hung up on him. His mother is watching him like a hawk, so he called Tom and asked him to ask Carrie to keep trying till she got through to me. Peter's father is back from vacation and he's coming here!

Dear God, I'm afraid. Dr. Winder is a horrible man. Even Peter hates him, and he's his father. He could kill Peter—he's that kind of person. Please don't let him come until after we're gone.

I was a nervous wreck all day. Carrie said it was prenuptial jitters, which made me laugh because the way she said the word *prenuptial* made it sound like she was sneezing.

I better stop writing. It's almost five-thirty, and I have to take a shower and get dressed before Carrie comes to pick me up. She says Dianne's coming tonight and so is Mark Miller. Lily isn't sure.

Everything's off. Peter is on his way to Santa Barbara. He called me from a pay phone at a restaurant where they'd stopped, just as I was getting ready to leave. He told me not to worry. He'll be back soon, and he's not going to let anything keep us apart. He loves me.

I hung up the phone and staggered over to a chair and sat down. I felt like I was being strangled. I couldn't catch my breath. All at once everything had changed. One minute I was getting

69

ready to go to a party with my friends to celebrate my wedding, and the next, Peter was gone and I didn't know if I'd ever see him again. I wanted to cry, to scream. It wasn't fair. It couldn't be happening. Not when we had everything planned. And then Mom called from the living room that Carrie was here. I didn't know what to do, so I went with Carrie. It was awful.

There were all of these things around reminding us that we were supposed to be having a party. The table was set with Mrs. Graham's best dishes. There were the flowers and all of this food that none of us could eat. Carrie's "wedding cake" with the bride and groom on top was sitting out on the kitchen counter.

I just couldn't face everyone. I asked Carrie to take me back home.

I feel so empty and tired, but I can't sleep. All I can think of is that we'd be on our way to Las Vegas now.

I took the wedding ring out of the envelope and put it on my finger. I keep thinking about what Peter said when he gave it to me. He said he didn't need anyone's permission to marry me. He was as married to me as he'll ever be. Is this as married as we'll ever be? I wonder.

Peter called this morning after Mom left for work. His father was so furious when he heard about us that he got in the car and drove straight here even though he'd just stepped off a plane. He came storming into Peter's room at one o'clock Monday morning. He dragged Peter out of bed, yelling that he'd die before he'd give Peter permission to get married. Peter said he didn't need anyone's permission—he was getting married and no one could stop him. That was like waving a red flag at Dr. Winder. Peter's brother and mother had to pull them apart to keep them from killing each other.

Then Dr. Winder said okay, if Peter wanted to be that way, two could play that game. Either Peter could go with him right now or he would stop sending Mrs. Winder support checks. He blamed her. He said that if she were ever home, Peter wouldn't be in this mess. What could Peter do? He couldn't hurt his mother and his brother.

Peter said I shouldn't worry. He's not going to let anyone keep him from marrying me. He'll be back home as soon as his father's cooled down, because his father's new wife doesn't want him living there.

All the time I've known Peter, he's told me what a mean bastard his father is. I always thought he was exaggerating, but he wasn't. I can't believe he'd make Peter choose between me and his family that way. I'm scared of what he'll do next.

Friday, August 16

Four days since he left. I've called Santa Barbara at least twenty times. I keep getting the answering machine. They must have gone away. I should call Peter's brother—he'll know what's going on.

Saturday, August 17

Peter called from a pay phone somewhere in Massachusetts. His father's trying to enroll him in some prep school, but Peter doesn't think he'll get in because it's too late—their classes are already filled. They are only talking to him to be polite because his father went there. He said he'll be home before school starts. He was telling me that he loves me when the line went dead.

What if he does get into prep school? I know he said that everything would be all right, that he'll be back and we'll be together. But I can't help worrying. Nothing has gone right for us so far, has it?

Mrs. Ikura has been looking at me kind of funny. I wonder if she can tell. She hasn't said anything. I've been wearing super loose clothes, so maybe she doesn't know. I can't afford to lose this job now.

I've been working and working on *The Lark*, and it still doesn't sound right. Sometimes I think I should give it up, but I can't. I have to do this. It's a challenge. My music is the only thing in my life that isn't a complete mess.

Mom and I went back to see Dr. Price this morning for my five-month checkup.

Although I dreaded going, I have to admit it wasn't so bad. It felt kind of weird—lying there with my belly uncovered, with this man I hardly knew bending over it, listening to my insides with this cold stethoscope. I could feel his breath against my skin. He let me take a turn listening to the baby's heart. I couldn't hear anything that sounded like a heartbeat, but I said I did.

He asked me if I had felt the baby move. I didn't think so, but when he said it felt like a butterfly fluttering, I realized I had. Then I had the ultrasound.

It was incredible! The nurse or technician put some sort of warm goop on my belly and then rubbed this plastic thing back and forth over it, and there it was on this television screen—a tiny baby. *My baby!*

Until the minute I saw it, and its tiny hand moved as if it were waving at us, I had never thought about it as a real baby. It was just something that was causing me trouble. But when I saw it, tears came into my eyes.

The technician was nice. "It really is something to actually see it," she said, like it was the most normal thing in the world to cry.

She asked if I wanted to wait to see if it would move so we could tell if it was a boy or a girl. I wanted to know, and at the same time I didn't. Anyway, the baby never got into a position where we could see. It doesn't matter. It's mine, whatever it is—mine and Peter's.

Now that I know what it's like, I keep feeling the baby move. It hasn't stopped the whole time I've been writing.

My dear little astronaut with your butterfly kicks, I love you.

❧ Tuesday, August 20

Mrs. Ikura asked me if I was pregnant this morning. I *knew* she would let me go as soon as she found out, and she did.

She said she'd thought I might be pregnant for a couple of weeks now, but she wasn't sure. She told me she was sorry to have to let me go because I've been a good worker. But she needs someone who can do a lot of lifting and carrying, and she doesn't feel that she can ask me to do it in "my condition."

I wanted to beg her to change her mind, but I didn't. I didn't say a word. I just bit my lip and nodded like I understood.

I didn't really like working there that much anyway, but it was a job and I needed the money. I'm going to need money even more with the baby coming—and who's going to hire me if they know I'm pregnant?

Wow! I just had an idea! What if I could give violin lessons to little kids? Mrs. Rykoff would know, but I'm embarrassed to ask her because I'd have to explain to her why I want to do it.

Sandy's friend Heather came over. They were talking about what classes they're taking next semester, and I wasn't really listening to them. Out of the blue, Heather turns to me and asks, "Are you going back to school?"

Her saying that made me realize that Mrs. Ikura wasn't the only one. Everyone can tell. I didn't know what to say to her because I hadn't been thinking about school at all.

"I don't know," I said.

"Oh," Sandy said in that know-it-all way she sometimes has, "of course she's going to school. She can't quit at the end of tenth grade."

"I don't know," I said. "I've been thinking about becoming a welfare mother and watching television all day."

She gave me one of her dirty looks and opened the freezer to see if there was any ice cream.

I forgot that school starts in two weeks. I can just see it now. Me coming into class every day, and everyone watching me get bigger and bigger, pretending they're not really looking. Some of them will feel sorry for me—they're the ones who will try to be nice, but not too nice. Most kids will act like I'm not there, like I'm some kind of subhuman. Wouldn't want to be contaminated by someone like me. I don't think I could stand that. It would be too hard.

I told Mom when we were doing the dishes that I wanted to quit school and get a job. Though I wasn't even talking to him, Daddy blew up. "Isn't it bad enough you got yourself pregnant? Now you're telling us you want to quit school, too."

First he tells me I have to have an abortion or go away because he can't face people, and now he tells me I have to go to school. He'll throw me out of the house if I quit. "I pay for the roof over your head and the clothes on your back," he shouted. "And as long as it's me who pays, you are going to finish high school."

Boy, he brings it up every chance he gets: "I'm supporting you, so you have to do whatever I say." I wouldn't take a nickel from him if I didn't have to.

It doesn't matter anyway, because I can't quit school until I turn sixteen, which isn't for a month and a half. But they can't make me go back to Irvine High, not even for six weeks. Even Daddy understands that. Mom's taking off work tomorrow to see if I can enroll somewhere else.

Saw Mrs. Garnet, my school counselor. It was humiliating. I knew it would be. Mom told her I was "...uh ... expecting." Mrs. Garnet said there was nothing to keep me from coming back to Irvine, but the district has a school-age mothers' program in downtown Santa Ana. I could enroll now, and after the baby came, the school would provide day care while I was in class. There were classes in child development and discussion groups about being pregnant and raising kids, too. It sounded okay to me. But I could tell from the way Mom's cheek muscle was twitching that she didn't like it.

Mom asked about home study, and Mrs. Garnet got all huffy. She said I'd have to have some medical condition that kept me from participating in regular classes and a doctor's letter to be eligible. She admitted that some pregnant girls did home study, but she's against it. "What you don't understand, Mrs. Larch," she said in that know-it-all way people like her have, "is that in home study, the girls aren't forced to confront the deep intrapsychic needs that made them get pregnant in the first place. It has been my experience that if girls like Valerie don't resolve those needs, they go right out and get pregnant again."

She made me so mad I stood up to go. But Mom didn't move. She put one hand over mine and made me sit down while Mrs. Garnet went on.

We decided that I would enroll in the school-age mothers' program for the time being.

Mom didn't say a word until we were out in the car. Then she exploded. She said she didn't want me in the program. She said it wasn't academic and I wouldn't learn anything in it. "It's designed for girls who are going to be nothing but mothers."

"What's wrong with being a mother?" I asked, which made her even madder.

"It's not funny, Valerie," she snapped at me. "Having a baby doesn't have to mean your life is over. That program is a dead end. It doesn't qualify you to go to college or teach you marketable skills—and take it from me, because I know from bitter experience, you're going to need to earn a living. Eventually you're going to have to be an adult. You can't be a teenager who got pregnant for the rest of your life. You have to look ahead. That's what Daddy and I are trying to tell you. That's why we don't want you to quit school. And that's why you're not going to keep this baby, if we have anything to say about it."

"You don't have anything to say about it," I said, and we didn't say another word the whole way home.

I was thinking about what Mom said about the school-age mothers' program being a dead end and about all the fun things I'd miss not going to school, like hanging out with Carrie and Dianne and all the other kids, and playing in the orchestra and being in school plays and the prom, and graduation. And I started to feel sorry for myself. I even began to think that she's right. I *am* too young to be anyone's mother. Then I had to stop and tell myself it wasn't the baby's fault I got pregnant. It's my fault for letting it happen—and Peter's.

Please don't take it personally, my little astronaut. I know I shouldn't feel that way about being pregnant with you. It's not your fault. But sometimes when I think about all the things I'm going to miss out on, I can't help it.

Yesterday Dianne asked me if I wanted to take a bike ride with her to El Moro Beach, "if it won't hurt the baby or anything." I said I couldn't go. Then today Arianna asked me to go to the beach with her. There was no way I was going to let everyone see me in a bathing suit, so I made some excuse. The only people I don't feel funny being with right now are Carrie and Nick. They've been terrific. Nick and I walked all the way to Penguin's after dinner the other night: five miles there and back just to get some frozen yogurt. And last night Carrie and I went to the movies. Afterward we sat in the car and talked.

She thought that it was a big mistake for me to switch schools. She said I was being paranoid, most kids wouldn't even notice that I was pregnant. But I said she was wrong. How could I go to swim meets or football games or hang around the lunch tables where the guys sit when I was expecting a kid? And what was I going to do once the baby is born? Take it to my classes? To dances? Parties? There's day care at the school-age mothers' program. And the other girls in the program are in the same boat. She said I was throwing away my chance for a decent education. She was starting to sound just like my mom, so I changed the subject and asked about her and Tom. She said she knew she should break up with him because of what he did when she was away, but she didn't want to because she still liked him a lot.

She asked me about Peter. I said I thought he'd be home soon, although I didn't know for sure.

"Haven't you spoken to him?" she asked.

"Not for a week," I admitted.

"He hasn't called for a whole week!" she yelled.

I told her that it's hard for Peter to call from a pay phone with his father watching him all the time and with my mother or father hanging up on him. The whole time I was saying that, though, I was thinking, why hasn't he called? What if he doesn't come back? Carrie must have read my mind, because then she asked me what I was going to do if Peter didn't come home. "I don't know," I said. "But he is coming back. He promised he would."

She drove me home because I had to go to the bathroom. I must go at least twenty times a day. The pregnancy books tell you that you're eating for two, but they don't tell you that you're peeing for two.

Carrie heard from Tom that Peter is going to school back East. She kept saying that it's only a rumor, Tom doesn't know definitely, and I shouldn't believe it until I hear from Peter. But I haven't heard from Peter, and I have this sinking feeling that it's true and he's afraid to call and tell me. Oh, please, God, let it not be true. Please let him come back.

It's true. Peter isn't coming back. He's been accepted at Westfield.

I felt like I'd been hit over the head with a hammer. I was standing in the kitchen looking out at the backyard when his brother called me, and everything went blurry. After I hung up, I staggered over to a chair and sat down. I couldn't think. My chest felt ready to explode.

Nick came in and asked me if I was okay. I opened my mouth to say something, but I couldn't. I just started sobbing and couldn't stop.

He can't be going to school there. He said he'd be back. He promised he wasn't going to let anything keep us apart. And I believed him. What am I going to do? I can't have this baby by myself. I feel so alone. I wish something would happen to it. I wish I were dead.

I can't get this book called *An American Tragedy* out of my head. It's about this guy who gets a poor factory girl named Roberta pregnant. Then he meets this rich girl and falls in love with her. So he takes Roberta out boating to drown her so he can be free to marry the rich girl, only he doesn't have the nerve to push her overboard. The rowboat overturns by accident, and Roberta drowns, anyway.

It's not that I think Peter ever wanted to murder me or anything like that, but I wonder if he's relieved things turned out like this. He can forget about me and go on with his life like nothing happened. Peter isn't a weasel like the guy in *An American Tragedy*. Still, you can't really tell about other people, can you? I was counting on Peter, really counting on him, and I shouldn't have. I couldn't help it. I didn't know what else to do. I don't know what else to do.

Dianne and I bumped into Mr. and Mrs. Rykoff today when we were coming out of the bakery. Mrs. Rykoff couldn't take her eyes off my stomach the whole time we were talking. I thought she was going to say something embarrassing about it because she always comes right out and says what's on her mind, but she didn't. She just asked me if I was practicing. I told her I was working on Vaughan Williams's *The Lark Ascending*. She said she was impressed, it's a hard piece. I told her I was finding that out.

She was wearing one of her costumes: off-the-shoulder ruffled blouse, a full skirt, ballet slippers, silver earrings dangling down to her shoulders, and a half dozen silver bracelets. Dianne was bug-eyed staring at her.

I'm sure Mr. and Mrs. Rykoff were clucking their tongues all the way home about how it's too bad I've ruined my life.

They're right. My life is ruined.

Dear Peter,

There's so much I want to say that I'm writing to you even though I don't know where to send this letter.

I miss you. I think about you all the time: your smile, your laughing golden brown eyes, your strong, straight back, your arms. I think about how we were together, too. How it felt to hold you tight against me, to move my body with yours—and I ache with longing.

Oh, Peter, I love you. You said you loved me, but I haven't heard from you for weeks, and I'm afraid that I'll never see you again.

I don't know what to think anymore. Am I a fool to believe your promise? Everything tells me that I am being blind and deaf to what's happening—everything but my love and my need to believe in you.

Valerie

❧ Sunday, September 1

I'm home alone. Sandy went back to San Francisco this morning, and Mom, Daddy, and Nick went out sailing in the harbor this afternoon. They didn't ask if I wanted to come with them—they just went without me.

I wouldn't care so much if Peter were here with me. And he would be if I weren't pregnant. Everything would be different if I weren't pregnant. Oh, God, I wish I weren't. Because there's this thing growing inside me, I am here alone. And I don't know what to do. I've made such a mess of everything. I hate myself.

This morning I went shopping with Mom. We bought a pair of overalls and a couple of oversize shirts and this maternity outfit with leggings and a big overshirt. It's a gorgeous color, a sort of lavender blue.

I promised myself I wouldn't take anything from her or Daddy that I didn't have to, but she kept nagging me, saying she couldn't stand my going to a new school in one of Nick's old shirts. When we got to the maternity department, the saleslady started showing Mom the slacks as if they were for her. "They're for her," Mom said, turning to me.

The saleslady looked down her nose at me like I had a disease. "Oh, they're for the young lady," she said.

I guess I should get used to it, but I can't. Nobody ever looks at my face when they talk to me now—they just stare at my stomach. Mom said that always happens when you're pregnant, no matter how old you are, but I think she said it just to make me feel better. It was really nice of her to buy me all of those things even though she hates my being pregnant. On the way home she tried, in a sort of roundabout way, to bring up adoption. I told her I didn't know why she brought it up when we were having an okay time together. Did she want to ruin it?

Had to catch the bus at six-thirty this morning to get to my new school. It's in a continuation school way over in Santa Ana. I was half dead by the time I got home this afternoon. I just flopped on the bed and fell asleep.

Mom was right. I'm not going to learn much there. The teacher, or whatever she is, looks like a baby doll, and her voice sounds like a little girl's. Mrs. Penny Zakos (that's her name) is oh-so-understanding and wants us to feel free to come to her with all our questions. I wouldn't ask her how to get to the girls' bathroom.

They haven't received my transcript, so they don't know where to place me. Not that it matters, since there aren't any real classes besides child growth and U.S. history. You work on math and English out of workbooks.

The other girls seem nice enough. Mostly I kept to myself. One Mexican girl (I think her name's Yolanda) who's very pregnant offered me half her sandwich at lunch because I forgot mine. I was very hungry, and it was nice of her to offer.

The babies were across the hall in the nursery. There were eight of them—two eensie weensie newborns in bassinets, two about three months old, another that was trying to get up on his hands and knees so he could crawl, a couple that were just learning to walk, and an older one that was trying to feed itself and getting food all over its face.

I watched the newborns for a while at lunchtime. They were asleep, and you could tell what they were dreaming. One of them was making sucking motions with its lips like it was nursing, and the other one was smiling like it had just heard the funniest joke. It was kind of neat.

Watching the babies in the nursery, it really hit me that I'm going to have a baby that sleeps and cries and nurses and wets its diaper. What am I going to do with a baby? I don't know anything about them. How will I take care of it?

Right now I hate Peter. I wouldn't be in this mess, if it weren't for him. I wouldn't be pregnant. Does he expect me to have this baby by myself? Does he even think about it at all? I doubt it. He has no idea what I'm going through or what it's like for me.

🌾 Thursday, September 5

Still working at *The Lark Ascending*. I'm not making much progress. It's really discouraging, but playing the violin is the only thing I do these days that makes me feel like myself. The rest of me seems to be disappearing behind this baby. It's taking over my mind and body like an alien invader. Soon the old Valerie Larch will disappear altogether, and in her place there will be a huge swollen belly with skinny arms and legs.

I GOT A LETTER FROM PETER!

I could hardly believe it when I saw his handwriting on the envelope. Lucky for me, the mail came while they were out. I thought I'd never hear from him again. But I should have known he wouldn't run out on me that way.

He wrote:

My blue-eyed love,

I haven't written to you or called all this time because I'm a coward, and I couldn't stand to tell you the bad news. By now you probably know that I'm not going to be back at Irvine this semester. They have me trapped here at Westfield, a prep school for spoiled rich kids whose parents want to get rid of them. I thought I was being so cool going along with my father. I didn't think I had to fight with him because I was sure I would never get into this place. But it didn't work out that way. Someone canceled, and they were oh-so-glad to have me—especially since my father was more than willing to pay full tuition and make a donation to their building fund.

I'm miserable, Val. I think about you all the time. I'm trying to find a way to get back for Christmas break so that I can be with you when the baby's born. I don't know how I'll do it yet because that s.o.b. took my car away, and I can't get my hands on any money. But I'll find a way, I promise. Until then, think of me: a prisoner here

*in this ivy-covered dungeon three thousand miles
away, guilty of the crime of loving you.*

I love you,
Peter

I love you, too, my dear, dear Peter with the
crooked smile and the laughing eyes. How
could I have ever thought you didn't care?

Dear Peter,

*I was so happy to get your letter, I danced
around the house all day. I never knew a piece
of paper could fill me with such joy.*

*I miss you. I think about you all the time.
Every time I pass someplace we used to go together, I get a lump in my throat. I love you.
I'm so relieved that you will be with me when
the baby is born. I've been so scared, Peter. It's
like I was walking around under this black
cloud. Knowing that you'll be home Christmas
has made the sun come out for me today and
tomorrow and the day after.*

*I'm okay. Our baby is okay, too. It is kicking
me right now. It kicks all the time—an overactive
kid, just like you. I wish you were here to feel it
kick. But you'll be back soon and then we'll be a
family—all three of us! It'll be hard. We'll be
together, though, and that's what matters. I don't
ever want to be separated from you again.*

*Please write. I want to hear everything about
where you are and what you are doing. If I can
picture it, you won't seem quite so far away.
Call me so I can hear your voice again and you
can hear me say I love you.*

Val

Carrie finally decided to break up with Tom. She told Tom their relationship wasn't going anywhere and she didn't want to go out with him anymore. The way she said it made me want to ask her where it was supposed to go. She didn't sound too broken up about it, but I am, even though I've known it was coming. The four of us had such fun together: like that time we drove to Rosarita Beach for breakfast,—and the time we all were skinny-dipping at Peter's and Mrs. Winder surprised us and we ran and hid in the bushes around the side of the house and had to stay there naked and shivering until she went upstairs to the bathroom, only then we almost got caught because Tom burst out laughing—and the time we went to that reggae concert and Carrie and Tom started the whole audience dancing in the aisles.

We were so happy. We thought nothing would ever change. Now look at us. It's not just my having a baby—it's everything.

I finally worked up the nerve to talk to Mrs. Rykoff about giving violin lessons to little kids. I was afraid of what she'd say. She was really nice about it, but she said I was a little young to give lessons and she was afraid most people wouldn't want to start with someone who was expecting a baby in a few months. She said if I was serious about it, though, I should put notices in places like the supermarket and the dry cleaners and see what happens.

Then she asked me how I was doing, and I told her what a hard time I've had with *The Lark Ascending*. She said that if I came over, she'd work through it with me. I told her I couldn't pay, but she said I should come, anyway. I couldn't stop thanking her.

Somehow, just knowing I'd be working on the piece with Mrs. Rykoff made me play better this afternoon. Even Mom said so.

Nick and I put up three-by-five cards in all the stores near the supermarket after dinner. I should put one up in the music store.

Today at school I met this girl named Stacy Mahoney. She's seventeen. A blond, big, sort of blubbery girl, but I think I'm going to like her. I was complaining about how hard it is to catch the bus at six-thirty in the morning, and she laughed. She said if I thought it was hard now, wait until my baby was born. Her Tyler is seven months old, and she has to change him, get him dressed and fed, and *then* get herself ready to catch the bus. She has to get out of the house by six every morning because her stepfather yells at her if the baby wakes him up. She's afraid he'll throw them out.

When I asked why she didn't get her own place, she looked at me like I was crazy. "You don't know anything, do you?" she said.

That kind of ticked me off, but as we kept talking about what it's like for her, I could see she didn't mean to put me down. I really don't know anything.

I *have* to get a job. I hate having to ask Mom and Daddy for every little thing. It's so demeaning. I can tell how they feel about me and the baby—like I don't deserve to live anymore because of what I've done. I asked at the dry cleaners, the stationery store, the bakery, and the deli. No one was hiring part-time except at the deli, and they needed someone to cover the lunch shift, not after school. It was so discouraging.

I mentioned it at dinner. Daddy said I was nuts to even try. "You can forget about getting a job with that load you're carrying. No one's going to want you."

Maybe he's right and I am crazy to think anyone would hire me. But why does he have to be so mean about it?

❧ *Thursday, September 12*

I made real progress on *The Lark* with Mrs. Rykoff. I was counting wrong. Now that I'm doing it right, it sounds a lot better. Mrs. Rykoff asked me to come and work with her on dynamics next week, which is really nice.

It turns out that Mrs. Rykoff had a baby when she was young, too—though not as young as me. She was in college and didn't drop out. She gave lessons, went to school, and took care of the baby, all at the same time! She thought I could do the same. Listening to her, I began to think, why not? If she did it, why can't I? It made me feel that it might be possible. I can't let getting pregnant stop me. I'd like to major in music the way she did. I'd have to work, but lots of kids work while they're in college—Sandy does and so does Heather. And Peter and I could take turns watching the baby, like Mr. and Mrs. Rykoff did.

Today we ignorant sinners in the school-age mothers' program were treated to the good advice of the county mental health worker. Her name is Mrs. Rosenshine, but everyone calls her Mrs. Rise'n'shine because she's one of those people who smile all the time and say things like "Now let's talk about it." She reminds me of my kindergarten teacher. Come to think of it, she had us all sit in a circle just like in kindergarten.

"I was in the nursery before coming here, and I noticed that Tyler was starting to crawl," she said.

"Yeh," said Stacy, "he's trying hard, but he keeps falling over."

"Keep your eyes on him—at this stage, they get into *everything*."

"Yeh, he's getting into stuff already," Stacy admitted.

"And how do you handle that?" Mrs. Rise'n'shine asked.

"Take it away from him. Tell him no."

"Slap his hand if he don't let go!" chanted Tiffany.

This led into an utterly fascinating discussion about putting things away so the baby can't reach them—a point that could be made in one sentence by most people, but not by Mrs. Rise'n'shine. She went on and on, during which time I wrote Peter's name over and over with my left hand to see how it looked, Debbie John-

ston got up and walked out of the room, and
another girl didn't even bother to whisper that
she admired the outfit of the girl sitting next
to her.

How these discussions are supposed to teach
us anything is beyond me.

I went to the movies in Newport Beach with Carrie, Dianne, Lily, and Arianna last night. Some guy was trying to hit on Dianne, and Lily was egging him on, even offering him popcorn. What a jerk! Everyone thought Lily was making an ass of herself.

It wasn't until I came home that I had a chance to think about how weird it was. I kept waiting all evening for someone to say something about Peter, but no one did. They didn't even ask about him. They didn't say anything about my not being in school, either. They were all s-o-o-o-o nice, s-o-o-o friendly and careful. It was like they were all pretending nothing's changed.

I wish they were right. But everything's changed and I can't ignore it. You won't let me, will you? You in there with the elbows and knees.

I got a long letter from Peter today. It was really bizarre. He wrote all about his school and his roommates and his classes. But he didn't say anything about the baby or ask how we were doing. It was like with the girls Saturday night—as if I weren't pregnant. He didn't say anything about coming home at Christmas, either. What if he's changed his mind about me and the baby? He's been gone so long.

What is the matter with me? He says he loves me. He wrote *Peter Winder loves Valerie Larch—I love you—Be mine—Peter and Valerie* all around the edges of the paper. He wrote that next to his bed he has a picture of me that he kisses every night. Does that sound like he doesn't love me anymore? But, if he loves me, why didn't he say anything about coming home or getting married or the baby? We have to start thinking about the future, to make plans.

I don't know what to say to him. I don't want him to feel like I'm forcing him into anything, but I've got to know when he's coming home and what we're going to do. The baby's due in three months.

Dear Peter,

What a relief to get your letter. I was really worried about you all alone in that horrible place. But now I know you're okay. I can picture your school and the dorm, the other kids— and everything.

After I read about all the new things you are doing, my life seems really boring. School is a drag. I don't remember if I wrote to you about it, but I didn't go back to Irvine, either. I couldn't stand people staring at me and talking behind my back. You should see how big I'm getting. Everyone can tell now, even Mrs. Ikura at the nursery. She fired me because she said she couldn't ask me to lift things in "my condition." Anyway, I got into this program for pregnant girls. Academically it's a joke, but at least nobody stares at me.

Your classes sound hard, especially trig. Mr. Hammond sounds like a Gestapo sergeant stalking up and down the aisles, but I can't believe he's even worse than Mr. Getsey was last year. Remember what he did to Tom? I always thought teachers at private schools were better than the ones we have in public school, but I guess not.

Your roommates sound like fun, except for the smelly one. That's obnoxious. Is he really that dirty? Has he broken down and taken a shower yet? Pew! Glad he's not my roommate. But I wish you were. It sort of sounds like you are settling in, which scares me a little, especially since you didn't say anything about coming home. I know you promised you would, but

I'm a little paranoid right now. I wish we could talk. I need to hear your voice. Can't you call?

I love you, Peter. I carry your image with me everywhere. At night I am with you in my dreams. During the day I can hardly think of anything else except you and what we did when we were together and what we'll do after you come home.

Remember when you gave me that poem and we talked about how everything seems more real when you're in love? I've been thinking about it a lot lately because I miss you and because nothing seems real to me anymore.

Please come home, Peter. I love you. I need you. Your baby needs you.

Val

I fainted today in school. I was concentrating on my English workbook, and I must have stood up too fast to go sharpen my pencil, because I blanked out and fell. I was so embarrassed. While I was in the back of the room lying down, Mrs. Zakos came to sit with me. She wanted me to see the nurse, but I didn't want to. Then she asked if I was getting prenatal care, and she made me promise I'll tell Dr. Price what happened. She really got me scared that I might be anemic or sick.

Oh, please, God, let my baby be healthy. I really don't want anything bad to happen to it. Listen, you little astronaut floating inside me, are you okay? Please be okay. I love you.

Mom took me to see Dr. Price this morning. I'm anemic and I need to take iron pills and eat more, but, thank God, the baby is okay. It's just a little small.

Afterward we went for a sandwich, and we had this talk. It was the nicest conversation we've had since she found out I was pregnant. She didn't lecture me or tell me I had to give the baby up for adoption.

"You're lucky you're having such an easy time of it," she said. "I was sick the whole time I was pregnant with each of you kids. Not just the first three months, but the entire time. My back hurt, my feet swelled up so I couldn't get into my shoes, and I had cramps in my legs that kept waking me up at night."

"If it was that bad when you were pregnant with Sandy," I asked, "why did you ever get pregnant again?"

She laughed. "I suppose you forget when it's all over. And besides, we wanted to have a bigger family."

I'm glad that she went ahead and got pregnant again or I wouldn't be here. But I can't believe you forget. I know I won't.

Went over to Mrs. Rykoff's this afternoon to work on dynamics. I think I made a lot of progress, which made me feel happy. At the same time, it made me sad that I'm not taking regular lessons. Sometimes, like today, when I'm playing well, I think I could actually become a professional. Mrs. Rykoff says she thinks I could.

On the way back, I stopped at a little sandwich place near College. They had a Help Wanted sign in the window, and I asked the lady behind the counter about working there. She said she thought her husband might have already hired someone, but she wasn't sure. It sounded like she might be trying to give me the brush-off. Still I should check back just in case.

Friday, September 20

We had Mrs. Rise'n'shine again in school today. She used my fainting on Tuesday as an excuse to lecture us about nutrition. She went on and on about how we were all eating for two and said that if we felt sick after big meals, we should snack all day—"grazing" she called it, like we were cows or something. It was so boring, I felt I ought to apologize to everyone. I was glad when she finally ran out of things to say about eating and turned to exercise. She went on about that, too, and how it could reduce the pain of childbirth. She made giving birth sound like torture. Stacy said it was for her. It hurt so bad that she wanted to die. I don't like to think about it. Dr. Price wants me to go to this prepared childbirth class at the hospital.

❧ Sunday, September 22

I've been crying and I feel awful, almost like I'm sick. I was supposed to go over to Lily's to make dinner and watch a video with her and Arianna. I've hardly seen them since school started, but Lily called just as I was walking out the door and told me not to come. She said her parents were having company, so I said they should come over here, since Mom and Daddy were going out. She said she couldn't. I didn't think about it until I talked to Arianna. When she said she couldn't come over either, I knew it was because of me. They don't want to be friends with me anymore.

❧ Tuesday, September 24

Carrie said I shouldn't be mad at Lily. It's not her fault. Her parents told her she couldn't be friends with me anymore. According to Carrie, Lily feels bad about it, but she can't go against them.

I don't care what Lily says—I know I would have stood behind her no matter what my parents said.

There was a baby shower at school today for Yolanda. I ended up buying an adorable little terry-cloth suit. But it cost twelve dollars, and that was on sale. Everything I liked was so expensive! A sweater, a tiny little thing, cost twenty dollars! I don't know how I'll ever be able to afford things for my baby. Stacy says she can give me stuff Tyler has outgrown. That will help.

The party was nice. The room was decorated with pink and blue crepe paper and balloons. There was pizza and stuff to drink, and Mrs. Zakos brought a cake decorated with a picture of a stork delivering a baby. It looked professional, but Stacy said Mrs. Zakos made it herself.

Yolanda's boyfriend, Felix, wants a boy real bad. They don't even have a name picked out for a girl. We all teased him about it when he came at the end of the party to pick her up.

"I only make sons," he told us.

"You might be surprised, Felix," Mrs. Zakos said. "There's a fifty-fifty chance it's a girl."

He laughed. "If it's a girl, I'll lock her up until she's thirty. I won't let any guys like me come around," he said. We all laughed because he's *definitely* the kind of guy parents don't want hanging around their daughters.

I can't decide whether I'd rather have a boy or a girl. Peter said he wanted a girl. I like Rachel and Lila for a girl, and Jesse for a boy. I also like the name Zachary, but I don't think

Peter would. He likes these prissy names like Will and Andrew and Elizabeth. I wish he'd call so we could talk about it. I mailed my letter to him ten days ago. He must have it by now. If I don't hear from him soon, I'll go crazy!

I ran into Tom at Penguin's this afternoon. He came over to sit with Nick and me. He was going on about how sorry he felt for Peter. And the whole time, I kept thinking, what about me? *I'm* the one who you should feel sorry for. *I'm* the one whose body is being taken over by this baby, and *I'm* the one in this dumb school-age mothers' program where you don't learn anything. Peter is in a fancy prep school having a wonderful time. Sometimes Tom really gets me.

But then I started thinking. Maybe I wasn't being totally fair to Peter. He didn't want to go away. His father made him. I keep having this daydream about him. Instead of writing to say he's coming back, he's decided to surprise me. And one day he's just there—waiting across the street when school lets out. I won't be sure it's him at first. He'll start to cross the street, smiling his wonderful smile, and then my heart will skip a beat because it *is* him. And he'll put his arms around me and bend over and kiss my hair like he never went away. I won't be able to talk because I'll be crying with happiness. He'll kiss my tears and say, "You're so beautiful. I love you. I'll never leave you and our baby ever again." And I'll laugh and say I *knew* that he would come back.

It probably won't happen that way.

I saw Lily at the drugstore this morning. She pretended she didn't see me. I felt awful. Afterward I was sorry I didn't go up to her and say something. We've been friends since seventh grade.

This baby is kicking the life out of me. I have to lie down. Nick wants me to go see this new vampire movie, and I don't want to disappoint him.

Mom and I got into a big fight today when we were doing the dinner dishes. She said Daddy and she had decided I should stop putting it off and go talk to Dr. Price about putting the baby up for adoption. Usually I tune her out because I know there's no use arguing. But she really got on my nerves. She was going on about how I had to be realistic, that I was too young to take care of a baby and it was irresponsible for me to think I could.

"What's irresponsible," I said, "is giving your own flesh and blood away. You can throw me out if you want, but you can't make me do that to *my* kid."

"Don't talk to me like that," she snapped. "If you want to be treated like an adult, you'd better start acting like one." And then she just glared at me with those awful blue eyes of hers.

I guess I was talking back, but I don't see how she can think it's so awful for me to keep my own baby. It's not like it was when she was growing up. Lots of kids have babies and keep them, too. It just shows how much she knows.

And the other thing that gets me is that she thinks I'm being a typical teenager and not thinking ahead. But she's wrong. All I ever think about is the baby and the future and whether we can make it on our own. I'm afraid we're going to end up like that homeless girl in the park last summer.

Today Mrs. Rise'n'shine asked what my plans are. They need to know if I'll be continuing with them next semester. I said yes, I'll be back at the end of January. Peter is coming home for Christmas and we'd be getting married, but I wanted to finish school.

"You mean lover boy is coming back from wherever?" Stacy butted in.

"Massachusetts," I answered, trying to stay cool.

Ruthie pressed her lips together and shook her head like she didn't believe me.

"Not every man is like Richard, Ruthie," said Mrs. Rise'n'shine. "There are decent guys out there. Maybe Valerie's is one of them."

Ruthie rolled her eyes and Stacy shrugged her shoulders.

I was really upset at first. Then I thought, why should they believe me? They don't know Peter.

🍂 Saturday, October 5

I don't know what to think. I finally got a letter from Peter today, and it scared me. It really did. He said nothing about coming home Christmas break, but he was all excited about applying to colleges back East:

> *Everyone is talking about where they're applying to college. My counselor advised me to put in an application to Hamilton as a safety school, in case I don't get into my top four choices. But I'm totally against applying there because it's in upstate New York, which is nowhere. I've been thinking about Princeton and Johns Hopkins. Maybe I'll try Pomona in California, even though it's not as good.*

Dear Peter,

> *Your letter really upset me. I know you didn't mean to scare me. I don't understand why you are even thinking of applying to places like Princeton or even Hamilton, for that matter. How can we afford it with the baby coming? I thought we'd both go someplace here.*
>
> *Please write and tell me when you're coming home, Peter. I beg you.*
>
> *We really need to talk about the baby and what we're doing, Peter. There are so many things that we have to decide. We can't just wait until you come home at Christmas. I've tried calling a couple of times. But it seems like*

you are never in your room. I don't understand why you can't call me.

Please don't be mad at me. More than anything, I want you to be happy. I don't want to keep you back. I don't want to ruin anything—your future or your life. But we have to be just a little bit realistic about what we can do. We can't just think about what we want. We have to think about the baby, too.

I love you. Sometimes I love you so much it hurts. I hope that you still love me and that you haven't changed your mind about us being a family. Please answer me right away because I won't breathe easy until I hear from you.

Love,
Val

Carrie and Dianne don't think Peter's coming back. I know they talked about it before they came to get me to go to the movies. The minute I mentioned his name, Carrie said, "You know Peter's not coming, Val. Why don't you face up to it?"

"How do you know?" I said. "He promised that he'd be home Christmas break, and I believe him."

"That doesn't mean he's coming to stay," Dianne said.

I tried to be cool about it. "He will" is all I said. "I don't want to discuss it, okay?"

They didn't say another word about it all evening, but I know what they think. They think I'm dumb to believe he'll come. Maybe they're right. Maybe he's not coming back. His letter really scared me. Still, I can't believe he would just leave me to have the baby by myself. He's the one who said we should get married. I didn't force him. I didn't say anything about it until he did. And he promised he'd be with me when the baby's born. I have to believe he'll come back. I can't help it—I love him.

Hurray! I have a violin student. One, which isn't a lot, but I'll have ten dollars a week I didn't have before. Although it's just a beginning, it makes me very hopeful for the future.

The little girl's seven years old, and her name is Sarah Najarian. She'll be coming a week from today. Mrs. Rykoff was too busy to take her on right now, and she recommended me. Mom said I could use the living room—I was a little surprised she didn't give me any grief.

I hope Mrs. Rykoff tells other people about me. I figure I'll need at least ten students just to be able to pay for groceries and diapers. If my parents would only let us stay here until Peter and I can find a place, everything will be fine.

Tuesday, October 8

Yolanda had a boy! His name is Esteban Ru-
dolfo, after her grandfather, and he weighed almost seven pounds. Felix must be happy. He
wanted a boy so bad. They took her to the hospital on Friday, but she didn't have the baby
until Sunday. She was in labor for thirty-five
hours, and then they had to do a cesarean because they were worried about the baby.

Debbie went to see her yesterday. She said
Yolanda was still sort of out of it from the labor
and the operation, but that Felix was the proud
papa, grinning from ear to ear. I can't believe it
took two days! I don't think I could stand being
in labor for that long. I'm such a coward when
it comes to pain. I have to see Yolanda and the
baby as soon as I can get a ride over there.

Wednesday, October 9

Tomorrow is my sixteenth birthday. What a
joke! I used to think all you had to worry about
when you turned sixteen was getting your driver's license.

I was hoping Peter would surprise me and call for my birthday. I thought at least he would send me a card. It's not like him at all. Last year he took me out to this restaurant on the beach for my birthday, and we'd just started going together then. I can't believe he forgot. No one else did.

Grandma and Grandpa Horvath called from Chicago. I didn't want to come to the phone at first because I was afraid they'd start lecturing me about how much I have disappointed them by getting pregnant, and then I'd start crying. But they were terrific. Grandma said she loves me and believes in me. "It's too bad this happened," she said, "but you are a strong girl, Valerie, and you will come through this. Don't lose your courage." It was so great of her to say that, especially when she's so sick. Grandpa was his usual self, telling me my music will carry me through, if I work hard at it. When I told him I was working on *The Lark Ascending*, he wanted me to get my violin and play it for him so that he could coach me over the telephone. I could hear Grandma in the background saying, "Don't be crazy, John."

Carrie and Dianne brought over a birthday cake after dinner, and even Daddy joined in when everybody sang "Happy Birthday" to me. Nick gave me a special reggae tape, and Sandy sent me this really funny card. I got two big shirts, which I really needed—a teal blue one from Mom and Daddy and a lavender one from Carrie and Dianne. Mom also bought me a CD of a young Israeli violinist playing *The Lark*. I didn't expect that at all.

Nothing from Grannie Larch, but then I know not to expect anything from her. Daddy says she'll never forgive me.

It would have been perfect if only Peter hadn't forgotten. While we were clearing the table, Carrie asked me if I'd heard from him, and I lied.

Peter did remember! I knew he would! His present came in the mail today. I was so happy that my hands were shaking and I was afraid I'd tear the card, which had a picture of a unicorn in a garden on it. He wrote:

My blue-eyed love,

Though we are bound by our love and not by chains, let this golden chain link us together on your sixteenth birthday.

Taped inside the card was this thin gold chain. It must have cost a fortune. It's incredibly beautiful. I'm so happy he remembered. I wish he had called, though. We have so much to talk about. I have to call Carrie. I'll bet she and Dianne change their tune when they hear about this!

Dear Peter,

I love it. The chain is gorgeous. I will treasure it always, because you gave it to me, Peter. It is a symbol of our love.

But, Peter, you shouldn't have spent so much money when we need every cent we can get our hands on. It is only two and a half months until our baby is due. I can't really believe it yet, but when I think of all the things we have to do to get ready, it seems like no time at all. And we haven't done anything.

126

My parents say that they won't let me bring the baby back here after it's born. That means we have to find someplace to live as soon as you get home. There's so much to talk about and decide, I wish you would call. Not being able to talk to you is driving me crazy.

I love you, Peter. Please forgive me if I sound distracted, but I'm scared. I feel so totally alone without you. Please call—I need to hear your voice.

Your present is wonderful.

Love,
Val

I'm going to be in a chamber group! Mrs. Ry-koff called and asked me to fill in for the second violin, who has a bad case of mononucleosis. I said I couldn't, but she wouldn't take no for an answer: "Ach, you must be wery busy these days, Walerie," she said.

"Not really," I admitted.

"Vell then, if you're not so busy," she asked, "vy von't you come?"

I told her that I didn't have any way to get over to her house because I couldn't ride my bike anymore. I didn't want to tell her the truth, which is that I don't like meeting new people because they always stare at my stomach and say dumb things like, "You're so young to be a mother."

And Mrs. Rykoff said, "That eez not a prob-lem. Somevone vill pick you up Vendnesday the tventy-third at five. Ve vill start vith Haydn, the *Emperor*. You vill go through it beforehand, ya?" And that was all there was to it.

I'm really happy that she asked me. But I'm scared that I won't be good enough. Everybody in the group is in college.

128

Today I taught my first lesson. It went pretty well, and I think Sarah really liked me. Actually, it was fun for me. Much better than working at the nursery. I showed Sarah how to hold the violin and the bow and let her practice bowing different rhythms. I'm teaching her to read music, too. We began with whole notes, half notes, and quarter notes, and clapping time. Next week I think I'll start her playing "Twinkle Twinkle, Little Star."

Mom was happy when I told her about the chamber group. She promised to find our tape of the *Emperor* for me to listen to before I start learning it.

I hope Mrs. Rykoff warns everyone about me so their mouths don't drop when they see me.

Stacy and I went to see Yolanda and her baby after school. The baby is beautiful. He has long, dark lashes and a perfectly round little face with lots of dark, straight hair. He makes me wonder what You-in-There with the elbows and knees are going to look like. If you take after me, you won't have much hair at first. But I know you will be beautiful, all little and cuddly and sweet.

When I asked Yolanda what labor was like, she shook her head and said, "You don't want to know." She and Felix had gone to childbirth classes, but they never expected it would be that bad.

I've been thinking about childbirth classes. Dr. Price and Mrs. Zakos keep telling me I should go, but Stacy says it's all couples. Everyone comes with a coach to help them when they are in labor. If Peter could come home at Thanksgiving instead of Christmas, it wouldn't be a problem. I don't know who else I can ask. Mom? Daddy? That's a joke. They can't stand the idea of my having a baby. It would be awful. Carrie? Dianne? They'd be more scared than I am. Sandy could do it, but she isn't here. And I would never ask Nick. I guess there isn't anyone.

Last night I dreamed I went into labor. I yelled for someone to come, but no one did. Peter wasn't there. When I tried to call Mom at work, her line was busy. I called Carrie, and she wasn't home. Neither was Dianne. Finally I tried Daddy. He hung up on me. The contractions were coming faster and harder. They were tearing me apart. I couldn't stand it anymore. The baby was coming! I woke up all wet and sticky. The baby was pummeling me with kicks.

I can't get the dream out of my head. What will I do if I'm alone when I go into labor? Call a cab? That's what Debbie says she's going to do. But what if the baby is born in the cab? It happens. I've seen it on the evening news. I think it would be awful. What if something went wrong?

Oh, Peter, why aren't you here with me? I need you. Please, please come home before the baby's born. Please don't leave us here all alone.

Dear Peter,

One of the girls at school had her baby last week, and she had a really hard time. She had to have a cesarean. I'm scared, Peter. I've been having nightmares about it. I keep worrying that you won't be here in time, and that I'll be all alone when I go into labor. The baby isn't due until the end of December—but it could be early. I am begging you to be here. I don't think I could stand to go through it without you.

I need you, Peter. Please call. I can't take much more.

I love you,
Val

Sandy came home for the weekend, and the three of us went to see this silly movie. Sandy let me drive, even though she's not supposed to because I'm not on the insurance. Nick wanted her to let him drive, too. She wouldn't because he doesn't have his learner's permit yet. I was a little scared because I hadn't driven since they found out about the baby, but I did okay. I'm so proud of myself. Sandy says all I need is a little practice, and I can get my license.

After the movie, Sandy took us to a great coffeehouse bookstore in Laguna. There was a classical guitarist. I ordered a *caffé latte* because it sounded exotic, but it was just coffee and milk.

This morning I found an old high chair for seven dollars at a garage sale. I almost bought it, then decided Mom would freak out if I brought it home. What I'm really going to need is a crib or a bassinet.

I wish I could get the baby a new crib. I'd love to have a white one—with those rounded, knobby slats—or maybe one that's a light natural wood. There are really beautiful cribs in the stores. But I'll have to find a cheap used one. The girls at school say you can pick something up at the Salvation Army.

I finally got a letter from Peter.

Val,

> *The last thing I wanted was to upset you. I bought the chain because I wanted to get you something nice for your birthday. I never thought you would make a fuss about the money I spent on it. The chain didn't cost that much. Not enough to make a difference.*
>
> *You think I don't care about the baby—like I'm some sort of flake. I don't need to be reminded. I think about the baby all the time. And I worry, too. I'm scared, too. But you know, Val, the baby is all you ever talk about in your letters. We can't stop living just because you're pregnant. What's wrong with my doing something special for you on your birthday? I don't understand what you're so upset about.*

I couldn't stop crying. It's so hopeless. He really doesn't understand. He isn't here and he can't imagine how fast the baby is growing. If he could see how big I'm getting or feel the baby move, maybe then he'd understand. But it isn't real to him. And all I can do is write.

Dear Peter,

> *I'm sorry I made you feel bad. The chain is beautiful and I love it.*
> *I was relieved you wrote that you think about*

the baby all the time. I was beginning to think I was the only one. I should have known better, but you never mentioned it in your letters before. I know you are afraid, too. Still, I really believe that the two of us can make it if we're together. We can't let this separation tear us apart. It's what our parents want, and we can't let them win.

Writing is so frustrating. We would never have had this misunderstanding if we were together. I can't wait until you come home at Christmas. I need you. I miss you so much it hurts.

Love,
Val

Went to see Dr. Price for my seventh-month checkup. He brought up adoption again. But he saw how upset he was making me and he stopped. He's been so nice that I had to explain how I feel about it. I told him just because I'm only sixteen and we don't have any money, it doesn't mean we don't love our baby. I could never have the baby, hand it over to some stranger, and forget about it.

Then he told me about these adoptions where it's not just giving up your baby and walking away. The mother knows the people who adopt her baby and can even keep in touch with the baby if she wants. I said I still wasn't interested because Peter and I were getting married. I thought Dr. Price was going to say something about our being too young, but he didn't. He just wished me luck.

I have to remember to thank Mrs. Rykoff for
talking me into playing with her chamber
group. I was really nervous when the guy came
to pick me up yesterday, but as soon as he
opened his mouth I forgot about myself. He
stutters so badly it took him a full minute to tell
me his name: Bret Arneson. Once we started to
talk about music, though, he didn't stutter at all.
Bret's a *really* good cellist. He was the only one
who knew the music. The rest of us were lost
most of the time. First violin is Gwen Matsuda.
She didn't have a chance to go through the
music beforehand, and she doesn't sight-read
very well. Even I knew the music better than
she did. Robbie Cohen, the viola player, picks
up on things quickly, and he was very impatient
with Gwen. He didn't say anything, but it was
easy to tell because he rolled his eyes every time
she messed up. Bret would be really nice-
looking if he didn't have this awful carrot red
hair.

I want to have my part completely under control next week. I love the music, and it's good
for me because it takes my mind off things.

Carrie called to ask me what I was going to wear to Dianne's Halloween party. When I told her Dianne hadn't invited me, she got all upset and said she was going to talk to Dianne.

"Don't say anything to her, please," I begged her. "I wouldn't go even if she asked me."

Carrie shouted at me, "Stop being such a damned martyr." Then she started lecturing me about how I was feeling so sorry for myself that I was cutting myself off from everyone.

Boy, did that make me mad! I told her off. It's not me doing the cutting, it's them. Dianne doesn't know how I feel about going to her party—she never asked me to come! She just doesn't want to be seen with me.

Now I'm so upset, I'm crying again. And it isn't because I want to go to Dianne's damned party. It's just . . . because.

I thought about it and decided Carrie was right. I need to stop cutting myself off. What I really need is to be with people who are going through the same things I am. So I asked Stacy if she wanted to do something tomorrow. I think she was sort of surprised that I called. She said she had to watch Tyler and her little brothers, but I could come over there.

I feel a little funny about going to her house. I really do like her, and she's been very nice to me at school. At the same time, I know I would never have anything to do with someone like her if I wasn't pregnant.

Hey, wait a minute. Look who's talking. . . . I'm not any better than she is. I'm an "unwed mother," too, and I'm younger than she is. Time to get real! I'm not Daddy's little princess anymore.

Went over to Stacy's. She lives in a teeny tiny apartment with her mother and stepfather and her two little brothers. She and Tyler have one bedroom, and her mother and Joe have the other. Her brothers sleep on the couch in the living room. I don't know how they do it, but they all seemed to get along. I tried to feed Tyler while Stacy was fixing supper for the boys. Every time I got the spoon in his lips, he closed his mouth and turned his head away. I kept feeding his cheek or his ear. He was a real mess!

Then Stacy's mother came home, and Tyler started bouncing up and down in his high chair and wouldn't calm down and eat until his Nana took over. He loves his grandma. Stacy says she takes care of him all the time. She's lucky.

When I told Mom how much Stacy's mother helps her, she said, "Don't get any ideas, Val. Just because Stacy's mother does something doesn't mean we will. We want something better for you and Sandy and Nick. If you insist on throwing your life away, though, you're on your own. We love you, but that's how it's got to be. I wish you'd listen to Dr. Price. He says he knows a couple who have been trying for years but can't have children of their own. They would love to have your baby, and they would give it the stable home it deserves. We can't afford to do that, Val. You know that."

They're really not going to help me. I guess I

always thought they'd change their minds, but I can see that they won't and I don't know what I'm going to do. What am I going to do? Oh, dear God, I wish I knew.

Dianne called. Carrie probably made her.

Sarah came over for her lesson today. She played "Twinkle Twinkle, Little Star." I like teaching her. And even if I say so myself, I'm not bad at it.

I saw Peter's mother. She came into the cleaners while the lady was making out the ticket for my clothes. My back was to her, and I don't think she recognized me. But I saw her in the mirror over the counter. I have nothing to be ashamed of, so I turned around with this big smile and said, "Hello, Mrs. Winder. How are you?" And she didn't even blink. She looked right through me like I was a piece of glass and walked out without getting her dry cleaning.

I don't know why, but it made me feel real good.

I can't believe it. Mrs. Rykoff nominated me for a scholarship to ProMusica. She called last night when I was practicing. I was so excited when she first told me that I was stuttering almost as much as Bret Arneson. It's such an honor. It's one of the best music camps in the country.

Then, when I was listening to her tell me about it, it hit me. What does it matter if she puts my name in now? I can't go.

I started to say so, and she interrupted, "I know, the baby. But I'm putting your name in anyvay. Let's just vait and see vat happens. If you get in, ve'll vorry vat to do vith your baby."

She said she'd help me get ready—I have to make an audition tape. It's incredible! I hope I get in, even if I can't go. It would be so great. Mom was really pleased. She kept telling me what an honor it was, as if I didn't already know, and that we had to call Grandpa. Then Nick came into my room and promised that he'd take care of the baby if I got in.

Daddy didn't say a word. He doesn't talk to me anymore. He doesn't even look at me.

Chamber group again. I didn't say anything about the scholarship, not even to Bret. I'm afraid talking about it will jinx it.

I've never heard anyone talk as much as Gwen does. She must know everything there is to know about Haydn string quartets—except how to play them. We kept having to stop because she was messing up. Robbie was really impatient with her. At one point this evening, he even said we should switch chairs. Bret and I laughed it off, but it's true, she's holding us back.

Even so, it was probably the most fun I've had all week. I love playing with them and wish I could be a permanent member. I suppose I won't have time once the baby is born. Oh, great, now I'm feeling sorry for myself! Sometimes, though, I just can't help it.

Dianne called again. I told Nick to say I wasn't home.

I finished doing my English already. The workbook is so easy, I could do it with my eyes closed. I can't wait until the bell rings and we can start our Halloween party.

Everyone is acting silly. I think it's because we are all wearing these ridiculous costumes. I didn't want to wear one, but everyone else did, so I felt I had to. I'm a jack-o'-lantern. It was Nick's idea. He said I was shaped like a pumpkin already— all I had to do was wear orange. I was mad at him for making fun of me, but then I thought: Hey! Wait a minute! It's not a bad idea. All I needed to be a jack-o'-lantern was to wear my green leggings and Daddy's old orange sweatshirt. I painted a jack-o'-lantern face on the shirt and stuffed it so that it's round in back, too.

Mrs. Zakos, who can be a witch, came as one, with her front teeth blackened and this green makeup all over her face and a real-looking wart on the end of her nose. Yolanda was a magician in a black cape and top hat. She dressed up Esteban in a bunny costume with long, floppy ears. He was adorable. She let me hold him for a while. He has these tiny little fingers and beautiful translucent fingernails. But what a grip he has! Yolanda took him from me when he started fussing. She says he's always hungry. He wakes her up twice during the night to nurse. She's exhausted.

Listen, You-in-There, you better not cry all night so I can't get any sleep. You won't, though. You'll be my little angel, won't you?

I've opened this diary every day for the past five days, but I couldn't write. Every time I read how dumb and trusting I've been, I started to cry.

Peter is never coming back and we're not going to get married. He says it's crazy for us to try to raise a baby by ourselves. We'll ruin our lives and the baby's if we try.

His letter was waiting for me when I came home from school on Halloween. I was still wearing that stupid jack-o'-lantern costume.

Dear Val,

I know it was my idea for us to get married and raise the baby ourselves. But I've thought about it a whole lot since I've been here, and I don't see how it would work. The way I see it, it couldn't be anything except grim. We'd always be broke. And what about the kid? What would it be like for him? The kid wouldn't appreciate it because he would never see us— we'd have to work all the time just to cover the rent. College? Forget about it! Who's going to pay for that? And what about my brother and my mom? If we got married, my dad would cut off their support. It would ruin everyone's life. I can't do that, Val. I guess you think I'm a liar and a coward. Maybe I am. But I'm just being realistic.

I don't know what you are going to do now.

146

And I probably shouldn't ask. I do still care about you and want to help. It's my baby, and I owe it to both of you. I have some money saved up, and as soon as I can get my hands on it, you can have it. It's not a lot—I'll send more when I can. It won't be much until I'm through medical school, but it will be something. Although I know it's selfish, what I can't do is give up my future.

It would be too much for me to expect you to understand my side of it. You will probably hate me forever. I guess I deserve it. But if it means anything to you, you should know that I am sorry.

Love,
Peter

He's gone. He says he loves me, but he doesn't, not anymore. You don't love somebody and leave her the way he's left me. He says he's sorry. But how sorry can he be if he's not coming back? He's going to go on with his life. He'll graduate from his fancy school, go to college, even go to med school. He'll just walk away as if it never happened. But I can't walk away, can I?

Can I?

I dreamed I was on the bus and there was this bundle on the seat next to me. I got off and went into a place that looked like Penguin's, and everyone from Irvine was there. They were all staring at me—for what seemed like forever. Carrie came over and asked me where my baby was, and I realized I'd left it on the bus. Suddenly I was racing down the street after the bus in a panic. Then I woke up.

Now I can't fall back asleep. I keep having these weird thoughts. I try to form a picture of the baby in my mind, but all I see is this bundled baby blanket, and when I open it up, there's nothing inside.

At lunch today, this girl whose baby is due the same time as mine was telling us that she and her husband were painting the crib they got from her sister. I had to leave the table because I was afraid I was going to start crying.

I haven't been able to think straight since I got Peter's letter. But I have to go on. I can't stay in my room and cry for the rest of my life. There's this baby growing inside me that wasn't there before, and I have to get ready for it. I can't just wait and let things happen anymore.

Stacy was right when she said I don't know anything. I don't even know what it costs to rent an apartment or to buy food. What if I can't do it by myself? What will I do then? Go on welfare? Where will I live? I have to be realistic and have a plan.

Hey, what about Grandpa and Grandma? They love me. They'd help us. And I could help Grandpa run the house and take care of Grandma. Mom says he's having a hard time. And Grandpa could coach me on the violin. Why didn't I think of this before?

Dear Grandpa,

This is a hard letter for me to write. I feel bad asking you for anything when you have every right to be ashamed of me. But I have nowhere else to turn. I'm desperate, Grandpa.

After the baby is born, can we come and stay

with you? I know that you already have your hands full taking care of Grandma, but I could help you with that. We could help each other.

I know I'm asking a lot from you, Grandpa, but I beg you to say yes. Please. I need you to so badly.

Love,
Val

🌿 Friday, November 8

I told Stacy and Debbie about Peter today. They said they'd gone through the same thing. Stacy's boyfriend hasn't given her a cent for the baby. Her parents want her to take him to court for child support, but she says he just lies around his parents' house and watches television all day and you can't get blood from a turnip.

Stacy offered to take me to look at apartments on Sunday. I'm hoping I won't need one. Still, I'd better find out how much they cost in case Grandpa says no. She said she'd take me to apply for welfare, too, but we should wait until right before the baby's due for that.

I felt a lot better after I talked to them. I still have to tell Carrie and Dianne about Peter. I already know what they'll say: "I told you so."

Went with Stacy to Santa Ana and Fountain Valley to look at apartments. There were these scary-looking men standing around the entrance at the first place we looked. I'd be afraid all the time if I lived there. The second one was filthy. The kitchen sink was stopped up, and there was garbage everywhere and awful-looking stains on the carpet. The third one looked like it hadn't been painted since it was built, and you had to go through the bathroom to get to the kitchen. I couldn't live there. But it doesn't matter, since the landlord wouldn't rent to me. When I went to talk to him, he looked me up and down and said, "I don't rent to kids."

Everything else we saw was even worse. I can't believe what those places cost. When I got home, I did a budget and discovered that I don't have enough money saved to live on even for a month. I don't know what I'm going to do if Grandpa doesn't say yes. I pray to God he does.

I told Mom I'd been looking at some apartments, and she said what she always says when anything having to do with the baby comes up: "Valerie, why are you doing this? I can't believe you really want to be on your own with a baby. You're only a baby yourself."

I said that they weren't giving me any choice. She accused me of twisting her words and said, "We never said that you couldn't come back here. We said you couldn't bring the baby home for us to take care of." I said it was the same thing. And she said she felt like she was watching me run across a freeway, and there was nothing she could do to save me. She looked like she was about to cry, and for a second I thought she's going to, she's going to give in and let me bring the baby home. She didn't, though. She just shook her head and looked away.

I feel sick after every one of these discussions. I keep hoping that they'll change their minds and say they'll help me. But it doesn't seem as if they ever will.

Carrie wants me to go shopping with her and Dianne today. The stores are having Veterans Day sales. I told her I didn't think Dianne would want me to come with them, but Carrie said I was being paranoid. We almost got into another fight over it. A few minutes after she hung up, Dianne called. She said she was sorry she hadn't invited me to her party. It was just that she didn't think I'd want to be there with all the kids from Irvine. I was very cool about it. She kept begging me to come with them, so I finally gave in and said okay. I have to face the two of them sometime, and it might as well be today. Anyway, I need a couple of things.

I told Carrie and Dianne about Peter. They didn't bawl me out. They didn't even say we told you so or anything. They were very sympathetic, but I know what they think.

Shopping was so weird. We were in Kids "R" Us looking at clothes and things, and they kept holding up all these expensive little sleeper things and oohing over them as if they were playing dolls. When I said I couldn't afford anything like that, they said, "Oh, but they're so cute." Then the two of them started whispering. The next thing I knew, they'd bought one for me. They could tell I wasn't thrilled about it. I guess I should have been more grateful, but my back was hurting and I kept having to go to the bathroom and I just couldn't take it anymore. Although I tried to make up for it on the way home, I think Carrie is still really hurt.

The Haydn is beginning to sound like something. I never would have believed it, but it really is coming together. Even Bret said that with a little more work, it might actually sound good. It makes me believe in miracles.

Bret wants me to be a permanent member of the group. He says Robbie thinks I'm pretty good, too. Robbie never says anything to me though, so who knows what he really thinks. Bret is probably just saying it to make me feel better. I'll miss him. I'll miss all of them, even Gwen. I wish I could do the recital with them, but the performance is only a week before I'm due. Their second violinist will be back the first week in December.

I thought Mom and Daddy were going out, so I told Stacy to bring Tyler over here this afternoon. She came just as they were leaving, and I couldn't believe how rude they were to her. Daddy acted like she wasn't there, while Mom didn't even introduce herself or say hello or anything.

Tyler was a handful. We couldn't take our eyes off him for a minute because he was crawling all over the living room. He got into everything, including the ashes in the fireplace and the electrical outlets. He put everything he found in his mouth. I was so exhausted by the time they left that I had to go and lie down, even though there were two of us watching him.

Afterward, all I could think about was how hard it is taking care of a baby. It made me really wonder, can I do it? Am I ready to be someone's mother? Or am I just fooling myself? I better find out before the baby gets here. Because it's one thing for me to wreck my own life, but I can't wreck the baby's life, too. That would be unforgivable.

I dreamed my baby was born with this tiny, tiny red wrinkly body and this huge monster head. It kept crying and crying, and I couldn't stop it. Then I was wide-awake, and Mom was sitting on the bed, saying, "It's okay, honey. It's okay."

Mom said a lot of pregnant women worry that their baby isn't normal, but that's not it. Something isn't right—I can feel it.

My Jewel,

I'm sorry to have to disappoint you, honey. You know I love you, but my first obligation is to your grandma, who is very, very sick. Even if Grandma were not so sick, I'm not sure that it would be a good idea for you to come here, dear.

There are times in life when we have to do things we don't like because there isn't anything else we can do. You should ask yourself if this isn't one of those times.

Listen to your Grandpa John. Right now, it seems to you that your life is over and everybody is against you. I am an old man, and I know that life is long and there will always be other chances. I know you hate the idea of giving the baby away. But, to tell you the truth, honey, it doesn't seem like such a terrible thing to me. Someday you will have a husband, and you will have other babies and you will be a good mother to them. But right now you are very young and in no position to take care of this baby.

You think your mommy and daddy don't understand and are being mean and selfish. But they love you very much and want what is best for you and for your baby. They may not be expressing themselves right because things are hard for them, too. Hear them through. They want to help you. Maybe together you can find the answer.

Don't be mad at me, honey. I love you and I am thinking of your future.

Your Grandpa John

He wrote that! My grandpa who tells me he loves me! I was so sure he was going to say, "Come. Stay with us. You're always welcome here." He's always telling me how much he loves me. "My Jewel," he calls me. I feel just like he punched me in the stomach. I can't believe he slammed the door in my face like that. Now I have nowhere to go. Nowhere to turn.

I read somewhere that you lose a lot of illusions when you grow up. I guess that's what it is. I must be growing up. I used to trust everyone. Like an idiot, I believed what people said. Peter said he wanted to get married, and I believed him. I used to believe that Mom and Daddy were big and strong and would never let anything bad happen to me. But something bad did happen, and when they found out about it, they didn't help. And Grandpa Horvath? He told me he loved me hundreds of times. And I thought he would do anything for me. But he won't even let me and his first great-grandchild stay with them for a little while. I believed them all. I shouldn't have. I was so dumb. I don't know what *I love you* means anymore. They're empty words.

❧ Tuesday, November 19

Last night I had this weird, mixed-up dream about my baby. I was standing all by myself in a valley watching this lark, which was my baby, soaring higher and higher over the hills on wings of sound until I couldn't see anything anymore because I was blinded by the sun.

When I woke up, I felt sad. So sad.

This girl came to talk to us at school today. She gave her baby up for adoption. Not that I think she was right to give her baby away, but I could understand how she must have felt. She was alone, just like me. Her boyfriend and her parents wouldn't have anything to do with her or her baby. She didn't have a job or any money. And she was really scared. What made me think it wasn't so bad was that she didn't just drop her baby and forget about it. She picked out the people to adopt her baby herself, and she got to know them. They were even with her in the delivery room when the baby was born. She goes to visit them and the baby.

Tiffany told the girl that if she had really loved her baby, she wouldn't have given it up. The girl asked her, "What kind of love is it to keep a baby you can't take care of or give a home to? That's selfish."

Is it selfish? I don't know anymore. It's your baby. Your responsibility. It's wrong to give your baby away. But is it right to keep it if you can't give it a home or take care of it?

At lunch today, we were all talking about the girl who gave her baby away. Most of the girls said she gave it up because she wanted an easy way out. I ended up taking her side. I was shouting, "What makes you think it's so easy? It's your own flesh and blood. Of course you want to keep it. You've been carrying it for all these months, feeling it grow and kick. You want nothing more than to take it home and watch it grow up. That would be easy. That really would be easy. But maybe it's impossible. Maybe that girl would have been on the street if she kept her baby. What kind of future is that to give a kid you love? If you love your baby, really love it, you can't just think about what you want. You have to think about the baby and what's best for it." The other girls all disagreed with me.

We were making the cranberry relish for Thanksgiving and Mom asked me if I thought that the baby was going to suffer. I had been telling her what the kids in the program said about the girl who gave her baby up for adoption. Then the telephone rang and I never had a chance to answer her, but I've been thinking about it ever since. I think the answer is yes, the baby will probably suffer either way—if I keep it or if I give it up for adoption. I don't know any way to avoid it. But what I keep asking myself is: Which way will there be less suffering?

I told Mom I'm thinking about giving the baby away. She took me in her arms and held me, and I held her and we cried and cried. It felt good not to be fighting anymore.

Dear Peter,

I didn't answer your last letter because I thought there was nothing more I had to say to you. But I was wrong. We are still linked, not by your golden chain, but by the baby we made in your room that day when we thought we loved each other.

I think I'm going to give the baby up for adoption. I believe that together you and I could have raised the baby, but I can't do it alone. I am responsible for the baby's being born, and the least I can do for it is to make sure it has loving parents and a good home.

For the adoption to be legal, you have to sign the papers giving up all claim to the baby.

Good-bye, Peter. I won't be writing to you anymore. I thought I loved you. I thought you loved me. But when you love someone, you want to be with them forever, and you want to make them happy. Neither of us were up to that. Maybe it was because we were too young. All I know is that I'll never feel the way I felt about you about anyone ever again.

Valerie

❧ *Monday, December 2*

I have an appointment at an adoption agency
on Wednesday. It is the same one the girl who
spoke at school went to.

I guess I can always not show up if I change
my mind. And I would cancel in a second if I
thought I could make it on my own.

I didn't know what to do with myself after I
made the appointment, so I picked up my violin
and started playing. I played *The Lark Ascending*
over and over and over again.